Gertrude

Chapter One

When I take a long look at my life, as though from outside, it does not appear particularly happy. Yet I am even less justified in calling it unhappy, despite all its mistakes. After all, it is foolish to keep probing for happiness or unhappiness, for it seems to me it would be hard to exchange the unhappiest days of my life for all the happy ones. If what matters in a person's existence is to accept the inevitable consciously, to taste the good and bad to the full and to make for oneself a more individual, unaccidental and inward destiny alongside one's external fate, then my life has been neither empty nor worthless. Even if, as it is decreed by the gods, fate has

1

inexorably trod over my external existence as it does with everyone, my inner life has been of my own making. I deserve its sweetness and bitterness and accept full responsibility for it.

At times, when I was younger, I wanted to be a poet. And if I were a poet now, I would not resist the temptation to trace my life back through the delicate shadows of my childhood to the precious and sheltered sources of my earliest memories. But these possessions are far too dear and sacred for the person I now am to spoil for myself. All there is to say of my childhood is that it was good and happy. I was given the freedom to discover my own inclinations and talents, to fashion my inmost pleasures and sorrows myself and to regard the future not as an alien higher power but as the hope and product of my own strength. So I passed unmarked through the schools as a disliked, untalented, yet quiet student whom they let chart his own course finally, because he seemed to elude the strong influences brought to bear upon him.

At about the age of six or seven, I realized that of all the invisible powers the one I was destined to be most strongly affected and dominated by was music. From that moment on I had a world of my own, a sanctuary and a heaven that no one could take away from me or belittle, and which I did not wish to share with anyone. I had become a musician, though I did not learn to play any instrument before my twelfth year and did not think that I would later wish to earn my living by music.

That is how matters have been ever since, without anything essential being changed, and that is why on looking back on my life it does not seem varied and many-sided, but from the beginning it has been tuned in a single key and directed solely to one star. Whether things went well or badly with me, my inner life remained unchanged. For long periods I might sail foreign seas, without touching manuscript-book or instrument, and yet at every moment there would be a melody in my blood and on my lips, a beat and rhythm in the drawing of breath and life. However eagerly I sought salvation, oblivion and deliverance in many other ways, however much I thirsted for God, understanding and peace, I always found them in music alone. It did not need to be Beethoven or Bach: it has been a continual consolation to me and a justification for all life that there *is* music in the world, that one *can* at times be deeply moved by rhythms and pervaded by harmonies. O music! A melody occurs to you; you sing it silently, inwardly only; you steep your being in it; it takes possession of all your strength and emotions, and during the time it lives in you, it effaces all that is fortuitous, evil, coarse and sad in you; it brings the world into harmony with you, it makes burdens light and gives wings to depressed spirits. The melody of a folk song can do all that. And first of all harmony! For each harmonious chord of pure-tuned notes — those of church bells, for example — fills the spirit with grace and delight, a feeling that is intensified by every additional note; and at times this can

4

enchant the heart and make it tremble with bliss as no other sensual pleasure can.

Of all the conceptions of pure bliss that people and poets have dreamed of, listening to the harmony of the spheres always seemed to me the highest and most intense. That is where my dearest and brightest dreams have ranged — to hear for the duration of a heartbeat the universe and the totality of life in its mysterious, innate harmony. Alas, how is it that life can be so confusing and out of tune and false, how can there be lies, evil, envy and hate among people, when the shortest song and most simple piece of music preach that heaven is revealed in the purity, harmony and interplay of clearly sounded notes. And how can I upbraid people and grow angry when I, myself, with all the good will in the world have been unable to make song and sweet music out of my life? Within me I can sense the urgent admonition and thirsting desire for one pure, pleasing, essentially holy sound and its fading away, but my days are full of mischance and discord. Wherever I turn and wherever I strike, there is never a true and clear echo.

But no more; I will tell you the story. When I consider for whom I am covering these pages — she who has in fact so much power over me that she can penetrate my loneliness and draw a confession from me — I must give the name of this beloved woman, who not only is bound to me by a large sum of experience and fate, but stands above everything for me like a sacred symbol, a star.

Chapter Two

It was only during my last year or two at school, when all my schoolfellows were beginning to talk about their future careers, that I also began to think about mine. The possibility of making music my profession and means of livelihood was really far removed from my thoughts; yet I could not think of any other career that would make me happpy. I had no real objection to business or the other professions suggested by my father; I just felt indifferent to them. Perhaps it was because my colleagues were so proud of the careers of their choice that an inward voice also told me that it was good and right to make a career of that which filled my thoughts and alone gave me real pleasure. It proved useful that I had learned to play the violin at twelve and had made some progress under a good teacher. The more my father resisted and worried at the thought of his only son embarking upon the uncertain career of an artist, the stronger grew my will in the face of his opposition, and the teacher, who liked me, strongly supported my wish. In the end my father submitted, but just to test my strength of purpose and in the hope that I would change my mind, he required me to stay on another year at school. I endured this with reasonable patience and during this time my desire became even stronger.

During the last year at school I fell in love for the first time with a pretty young girl who was in our circle of friends. Without seeing her often and also without strongly seeking her company, I suffered and enjoyed the emotions of first love as in a dream. During this period when I was thinking about my music as much as about my beloved and could not sleep at night because of my great excitement, I consciously retained for the first time melodies that occurred to me. They were two short songs and I tried to write them down. This made me feel shy but also gave me acute pleasure, and I almost forgot my youthful pangs of love. Meantime, I learned that my beloved took singing lessons and I was very eager to hear her sing. After some months my wish was fulfilled at an evening gathering at my parents' house. The pretty girl was asked to sing. She resisted strongly but finally had to give in and I waited with great excitement. A gentleman accompanied her on our humble little piano; he played a few bars and she began. She sang badly, very badly, and while she was still singing, my dismay and torment changed into sympathy, then into humor, and from then on I was no longer in love with her.

I was patient and not altogether indolent, but I was not a good scholar, and during my last year at school I made very little effort. This was not due to laziness and my infatuation, but to a state of youthful daydreaming and indifference, a dullness of senses and intellect that was only now and then suddenly and powerfully pierced when one of the wonderful hours of premature creative desire enveloped me like ether. I then felt as if I were surrounded by a rarefied, crystal-clear atmosphere in which dreaming and vegetating were not possible and where all my senses were sharpened and on the alert. Little was produced during those hours, perhaps ten melodies and several rudimentary harmonic arrangements, but I will never forget the rarefied, almost cold atmosphere of that time and the intense concentration required to give a melody the proper, singular, no longer fortuitous movement and solution. I was not satisfied with these meager achievements and never considered them as either valid or good, but it became clear to me that there would never be anything as desirable and important in my life as the return of such hours of clarity and creativeness.

At the same time I also had periods of daydreaming when I improvised on the violin and enjoyed the intoxication of fleeting impressions and exalted moods. I soon knew that this was not creativeness but just playing and running riot, against which I had to guard. I realized that it was one thing to indulge in daydreaming and intoxicating hours and another to wrestle strenuously and resolutely with the secrets of form as if with fiends. I also partly realized at that time that true creativity isolates one and demands something that has to be subtracted from the enjoyment of life.

At last I was free. My school days were behind me. I had said goodbye to my parents and had begun a new life as a student at the School of Music in the capital. I commenced this new phase with great expectations and was convinced that I would be a good scholar at the School of Music. However, to my embarrassed astonishment, this did not prove to be the case. I had difficulty keeping up with the great variety of courses I was forced to take. I found the piano lessons nothing but a great trial, and I soon saw my whole course of study looming before me like an unscalable mountain. Of course I did not think of giving in, but I was disillusioned and disconcerted. I now saw that with all my modesty I had considered myself some kind of a genius and had considerably underestimated the toils and difficulties encountered along the path to an art. Moreover, my composing was seriously affected, for I now saw mountains of difficulties and rules in the smallest exercise. I learned to mistrust my sensibilities entirely and no longer knew whether I possessed any talent. So I became resigned, humble and sad. I did my work very much as I would have done in an office or in another sphere, diligently but without pleasure. I did not dare complain, least of all in the letters that I sent home, but continued in secret disillusionment along the path I had commenced and hoped to become at least a good violinist. I practiced continually and bore hard words and sarcasm from the teachers. I saw many others, whom I would not have believed capable of it, make progress easily and receive praise, and my goal became even more humble. For, even with the violin, things were not going so well that I could feel proud and perhaps think of becoming a virtuoso. If I worked hard, it looked as if I might at least become a proficient violinist who could play a modest part in some small orchestra, without disgrace and without honor, and earn my living by it.

So this period for which I had yearned so much and which had promised everything to me was the only one in my life when I traveled joyless paths abandoned by the spirit of music and lived through days that had no meaning and rhythm. Where I had sought pleasure, exaltation, radiance and beauty, I found only demands, rules, difficulties, tasks and trials. If a musical idea occurred to me, it was either banal and imitative, or it was apparently in contradiction with all the laws of music and thus was bound to be worthless. So I said farewell to all my great hopes. I was one of thousands who had approached the art with youthful confidence and whose powers had fallen short of his aspirations.

This impasse lasted about three years. I was now over twenty years old. I had apparently failed in my vocation and continued following the course I had started only out of a feeling of shame and duty. I did not know anything more about music, only about finger exercises, difficult tasks, contradictions in the theory of harmony, and tedious piano lessons from a sarcastic teacher who saw in my efforts a waste of time.

If the old ideal had not secretly been alive in me, I could have enjoyed myself during those years. I was free and had friends. I was a good-looking and healthy young man, the son of well-to-do parents. For short periods I enjoyed it all; there were pleasant days, flirtations, carousing and holidays. But it was not possible for me to console myself in this way, to lay aside my obligations for a short time and above all to enjoy my youth. Without really knowing it, in unguarded hours I still looked longingly at the fallen star of creative art, and it was impossible for me to forget and stifle my feelings of disillusionment. Only once was I really successful in doing so.

It was the most foolish day of my foolish youth. I was then pursuing a girl who was studying under the famous singing teacher, H. Both she and I seemed to share the same predicament; she had arrived with great hopes, had found strict teachers, was unused to the work, and finally thought she was going to lose her voice. She took the easy way out, flirted with her colleagues and knew how to make all of us chase her. She had the vivacious, gaudy type of beauty that soon fades.

This pretty girl, Liddy, captivated me with her ingenuous coquetry whenever I saw her. I never stayed in love with her for long. Often I completely forgot her, but whenever I was with her, my infatuation returned. She toyed with me as she did with others, enticing me and enjoying her power, but she was only indulging the sensual curiosity of her youth. She was very pretty, but only when she spoke and moved, or laughed with her deep warm voice, or danced or was amused at the jealousy of her admirers. Whenever I returned home from a party where I had seen her, I used to laugh at myself and realize that it was impossible for a person of my nature to be seriously in love with this pleasant, lighthearted girl. Sometimes, however, with a gesture or a friendly whispered word, she was so successful in exciting me that for half the night I would loiter with ardent feelings near the house where she lived.

I was then going through a phase of wildness and half-willful bravado. After days of depression and dullness, my youth demanded stormy emotions and excitement and I went with other companions of my own age in search of diversion. We passed for jolly, unruly, even dangerous rioters, which was untrue of me, and we enjoyed a doubtful but pleasant heroic reputation with Liddy and her small circle. How many of these urges could be attributed to genuine youthful abandon, and how many were a desire for forgetfulness, I cannot now decide, for I long ago completely outgrew these phases of exhibitionistic youthfulness. If I indulged in excesses, I have since atoned for them.

One winter's day when we were free, we went on an excursion to the outskirts of the town. There were eight or ten young people, among them Liddy and three girlfriends. We had toboggans, whose use was considered exclusively a childhood pleasure at that time; and we looked for good slides in the hilly districts outside the town, on the roads and on the slopes of fields. I remember that day very well. It was moderately cold; at times the sun would appear for about a quarter of an hour and there was a wonderful smell of snow in the strong air. The girls looked lovely in their bright clothes against the white background; the sharp air was intoxicating and this energetic exercise in the fresh air was delightful. Our little party was in very high spirits; there was much familiarity and chaffing, which was answered with snowballs and led to short battles until we were all hot and covered with snow. Then we had to stop awhile to recover our breath before we began again. A large snow castle was built and besieged, and every so often we tobogganed down the slopes.

At midday, when we were formidably hungry from romping about, we looked for and found a village with a good inn; we cooled off, took possession of the piano, sang, shouted, and ordered wine and beer. Food was brought and enjoyed enormously, and there was good wine in abundance. Afterward the girls asked for coffee while we sampled liqueurs. There was such a festive uproar in the little room that we were all giddy. All the time I was with Liddy, who, in a gracious mood, had chosen me for special favor that day. She was at her best in this intoxicating and merry atmosphere; her lovely eyes sparkled and she permitted many half-bold, half-timid endearments. We played a game of forfeits, in which the forfeiters were released after being made to imitate one of our teachers at the piano, or after the number and quality of their kisses were adjudged acceptable.

When we left the inn and set off home, in high spirits and with much noise, it was still early afternoon but it was already growing a little dark. We again romped through the snow like carefree children, returning to town without haste in the gradually approaching evening. I managed to remain by Liddy's side as her companion, not without opposition from the others. I pulled the toboggan for stretches with her as rider, and protected her to the best of my ability against renewed snowball attacks. Finally, we were left alone; each girl found a male companion, and the two young men who were left without girls walked alongside, kidding everyone and engaging in mock belligerence. I had never been so excited and madly in love as I was at that time. Liddy had taken my arm and allowed me to draw her close to me as we moved along. She was soon chattering away; then she became silent and, it appeared to me, content to be at my side. I felt very ardent and was

19

determined to make the most of this opportunity and maintain this friendly, delightful state of affairs as long as possible.

No one had any objection when I suggested another detour shortly before reaching town. We turned on to a lovely road that ran high above the valley in a semicircle, rich in extensive views over the valley, river and town, which, in the distance, was already aglow with rows of bright lamps and thousands of rosy lights. Liddy still hung on my arm and let me talk, received my ardent advances with amusement and yet seemed very excited herself. But when I tried to draw her gently to me and kiss her, she freed herself and moved away.

"Look," she cried, taking a deep breath, "we must toboggan down that field! Or are you afraid, my hero?"

I looked down and was astonished, for the slope was so steep that for the moment I was really afraid at the thought of such a daring ride.

"Oh, no," I said nonchalantly. "It is already much too dark."

She immediately began to mock and provoke me, called me a coward and said she would ride down the slope alone if I was too fainthearted to come with her.

"We shall overturn, of course," she said laughing, "but that is the most amusing part of tobogganing."

She provoked me so much that I had an idea.

"Liddy," I said softly, "we'll do it. If we overturn, you can rub snow over me, but if we go down all right, then I want my reward."

She just laughed and sat down on the toboggan. I looked at her face; it was bright and sparkling. I took my place in the front, told her to hold tight to me, and, as we set off, I felt her clasp me and cross her hands on my chest. I wanted to shout something back to her but I could no longer do so. The slope was so steep that I felt as if we were hurtling through the air. I immediately tried to put both feet on the ground in order to pull up or even overturn, for suddenly I was terrible worried about Liddy. However, it was too late. The toboggan whizzed uncontrollably down the hill. I was aware of a cold, biting mass of churned-up snow in my face. I heard Liddy cry out anxiously — then no more. There was a tremendous blow on my head as if from a sledge-hammer; somewhere there was a severe pain. My last feeling was of being cold.

With this brief and frenzied toboggan ride, I atoned for all my youthful overexuberance and foolhardiness. After it was over, among many other things my love of Liddy had also evaporated.

I was spared the tumult and agitation which took place after the accident. For the others it was a painful time. They had heard Liddy shout out and they laughed and teased from above in the darkness. Finally, they realized that something was wrong and climbed laboriously down to us. It took a little while for them to calm down and really understand the true situation. Liddy was pale and half unconscious, but quite unharmed; only her gloves were torn and her delicate white hands were a little bruised and bleeding. They carried me away thinking I was dead. At a later date I looked in vain for the apple or pear tree into which the toboggan had crashed and broken my bones

It was thought that I had a serious concussion but matters were not quite so bad. My head and brain were indeed affected and it was a long time before I regained consciousness in the hospital, but the wound healed and my brain was unharmed. On the other hand, my left leg, which was broken in several places, did not fully heal. Since that time I have been a cripple who can only walk with a limp, who cannot stride along or even run and dance. My youth was thus unexpectedly directed along a path to quieter regions, along which I traveled not without a feeling of shame and resistance. But I did go along it and sometimes it seems to me that I would not willingly have missed that toboggan ride and its effect on my life.

I confess that I think less about the broken leg than about the other consequences of the accident, which were far happier. Whether it can be attributed to the accident, the shock and the glimpse into darkness, or the long period of lying in bed, being quiet for months and thinking things over, the course of treatment proved beneficial to me.

The beginning of that long period of lying in bed — say, the first week — has quite vanished from my memory. I was unconscious a great part of the time, and even when I finally recovered full consciousness, I was weak and listless. My mother arrived and every day sat faithfully beside my bed in the hospital. When I looked at her and spoke a few words, she seemed calm and almost cheerful, although I learned later that she was very worried about me, not for my life but for my reason. Sometimes we chatted for a long time in the quiet little hospital room. Yet our relationship had never been very warm. I had always been closer to my father. Sympathy on her part and gratitude on mine made us more understanding and inclined to draw closer, but we had both waited too long and had become too accustomed to a mutual *laisser faire* for awakening affection to show itself in our conversation. We were glad to be together and left some things unspoken. She was again my mother who saw me lying ill and could care for me, and I saw her once again through a boy's eyes and for a time forgot everything else. To be sure, the old relationship was resumed later and we used to avoid talking much about this period of sickness, for it embarrassed us both.

Gradually I began to realize my position, and as I had recovered from the fever and seemed peaceful, the doctor no longer kept the news from me that I would have a permanent memento as a result of my fall. I saw my youth, which I had scarcely begun to enjoy consciously, grievously cut short and impoverished. I had plenty of time in which to appreciate the situation, as I was bedridden for another three months.

I then tried hard to grasp my situation and visualize the shape of my future life, but I did not make much progress. Too much thinking was still not good for me. I soon became tired and sank into a quiet reverie, by which nature protected me from anxiety and despair and compelled me to rest in order to recover my health. The thought of my misfortune tormented me frequently, often half through the night, without my finding anything in my predicament to console me.

Then one night I awakened after a few hours of peaceful slumber. It seemed to me that I had had a pleasant dream and I tried in vain to recall it. I felt remarkably well and at peace, as if all unpleasant things were surmounted and behind me. And as I lay there thinking and feeling light currents of health and relief pervade me, a melody came to my lips almost without any sound. I began to hum it and unexpectedly, music, which had so long been a stranger, came back to me like a suddenly revealed star, and my heart beat to its rhythm, and my whole being blossomed and inhaled new, pure air. It did not reach my consciousness; I just felt its presence and it penetrated my being gently, as if melodious choirs were singing to me in the distance.

With this inwardly refreshed feeling I fell asleep again. In the morning I was in a good humor and free from depression, which I had not been for a long time. My mother noticed it and asked what was making me feel happy. I reflected awhile and then said that I had not thought about my violin for a long time; but now I suddenly did and it gave me pleasure.

"But you will not be able to play for a long time yet," she said in a somewhat worried tone.

"That does not matter — nor does it matter if I never play again."

She did not understand and I could not explain to her. But she noticed that things were going better with me and that nothing ominous lurked beneath this unfounded cheerfulness. After a few days she cautiously mentioned the matter again.

"How are you progressing with your music? We almost believed that you were tired of it and your father has spoken to your teachers about it. We do not want to persuade you, least of all just now . . . but we do feel that if you have made a mistake and would rather give it up, you should do so and not continue out of a feeling of defiance or shame. What do you think?"

I again thought about the long period of my alienation and disillusionment with music. I tried to tell my mother what it had been like and she seemed to understand. I thought I now saw my goal clearly again and I would not, at all events, run away from it but finish my studies. That is how things remained for the time being. In the depths of my soul, where my mother could not penetrate, there was sweet music. Whether or not I should now have my luck with the violin, I could again hear the world resound as if it were a work of art and I knew that outside music there was no salvation for me. If my condition never permitted me to play the violin again, I would resign myself to it, perhaps consider another career or even become a merchant; it was not so important. As a merchant, or anything else, I would not be any less sensitive to music or live and breathe less through music. I would compose again! It was not, as I had said to my mother, the thought of my violin that made me happy, but the intense desire to make music, to create. I again often felt the clear vibrations of a rarefied atmosphere, the concentration of ideas, as I had previously in my best hours, and I also felt that the misfortune of a crippled leg was of little importance beside it.

From that time on I was victorious, and however often since then my desires have traveled into regions of physical fitness and youthful pleasures, and however often I have hated and cursed my crippled state with bitterness and a deep sense of shame, it has not been beyond my power to bear this load; there has been something there to console and compensate me.

Occasionally my father came down to see me and, one day, as I continued to improve, he took my mother home with him again. For the first few days I felt rather lonely, and also rather ashamed that I had not talked more affectionately to my mother and taken more interest in her thoughts and cares. But my other emotion was so vivid that these thoughts about good intentions and feelings of compassion receded into the background.

Then unexpectedly someone came to visit me who had not ventured to do so while my mother was there. It was Liddy. I was very surprised to see her. For the first moment I entirely forgot how close I had been to her recently and how deeply in love. She came in a state of great embarrassment, which she disguised very badly. She had been afraid of my mother and even a law suit, for she knew she was responsible for my misfortune, and only gradually realized that things were not so bad and that the matter was really not her concern. She breathed freely again but could not conceal a feeling of slight disappointment. The girl, despite her troubled conscience, had in her feminine heart deeply enjoyed the whole business with its heart-rending and touching consequences. She even used the word "tragic" several times, at which I could hardly conceal a smile. She had not really been prepared to see me so cheerful and so little concerned about my crippled leg. She had had it in mind to ask my forgiveness, the granting of which, she thought, would have given me, her beloved, tremendous satisfaction, so that at the climax of this stirring scene she would have triumphantly conquered my heart anew.

It was indeed no small relief to the foolish girl to see me so contented and to find herself free from all blame and accusation. However, this relief did not make her feel happy, and the more her conscience was eased and her anxiety removed, the quieter and cooler did I see her become. Subsequently, it hurt her not a little that I regarded her part in the affair as so slight and indeed even seemed to have forgotten it, that I had quenched her apology and all the emotion and ruined the whole pretty scene. Moreover, and despite my extreme politeness, she realized that I was no longer in love with her, and that was the worst thing of all. Even if I had lost my arms and legs, I should still have been an admirer of hers, whom indeed she did not love and who had never given her any pleasure, but if I had been wretchedly lovesick, it would have been a greater source of satisfaction to her. That was not the case as she so well observed, and I saw the warmth and interest on the pretty face of the sympathetic visitor gradually grow less and disappear. After an effusive farewell, she finally went away and never came again, though she faithfully promised to do so.

However painful it was to me and however much it reflected on my power of judgment to see my previous infatuation sink into insignificance and become laughable, the visit did in fact do me good. I was very surprised to see this attractive girl for the first time without passion and without rose-colored spectacles, and to realize that I had not known her at all. If someone had shown me the doll I had embraced and loved when I was three years old, the lack of interest and change of feeling could not have surprised me more than in this case, when I saw as a complete stranger this girl whom I had so strongly desired a few weeks earlier.

Of the companions who were present at that Sunday outing in the winter, two visited me several times, but we found little to talk about. I saw how relieved they were when I improved, and I asked them not to bring me any more gifts. We did not meet again later. It was a strange business and it made a sad and curious impression on me; everything that had belonged to me in these earlier years of my life went from me and became alien and lost to me. I suddenly saw how sad and artificial my life had been during this period, for the loves, friends, habits, and pleasures of these years were discarded like badly fitting clothes. I parted from them without pain and all that remained was to wonder that I could have endured them so long.

I was surprised to receive another visitor to whom I had never given a thought. That strict and ironic gentleman, my piano teacher, came to see me one day. Holding his walking-stick and wearing gloves, he spoke in his usual sharp, almost biting tones, called the ill-fated toboggan ride "that women's ride business," and by the tone of his words seemed to feel that my ill-luck was well-deserved. All the same, it was remarkable that he had come, and he also showed, though he did not change his tone of voice, that he had not come with bad intentions, but to tell me that despite my general awkwardness he considered me a passable student. His colleague, the violin teacher, was of the same opinion and they therefore hoped I would soon return fit and well and give them pleasure. Although this speech almost sounded like an apology for previous harsh treatment and was delivered in the same sharp tones, it was as sweet to me as a declaration of love. I gratefully held out my hand to the unpopular teacher and, in order to show confidence in him, I tried to explain the course of my life during these years and how my old attitude toward music was beginning to return.

The professor shook his head and his voice whistled with derision as he said: "So a composer is what you want to become?"

"If possible," I said disheartened.

"Well, I wish you luck. I thought you would now resume practicing with fresh enthusiasm, but if you want to compose, you don't, of course, need to do that."

"Oh, I didn't mean that."

"What then? You know, when a music student is lazy and doesn't like hard work, he always takes up composing. Anyone can do that, and each one, of course, is a genius."

"I really don't mean that at all. Shall I become a pianist then?"

"No, my dear friend, you could never become that — but you could become a reasonably good violinist."

"I wish to do that, too!"

"I hope you mean it. Well, I must not stay any longer. Hope you will soon be better. Goodbye."

Thereupon he went away and left me with a feeling of amazement. I had thought very little about the return to my studies. Now I became afraid things would be difficult and go wrong again and that everything would be as it had been before, but these thoughts did not remain with me long, and it also seemed as if the grumpy professor's visit was well-meant and a sign of sincere good will.

After I had sufficiently recovered my health, it was intended that I should go away for a period of convalescence, but I preferred to wait until the usual vacation. I wished to return to work immediately. I then experienced for the first time what an astonishing effect a period of rest can have, particularly a compulsory one. I began my studies and my practicing with mistrust, but everything now went better than before. To be sure, I now fully realized that I would never become a virtuoso, but in my present mood this did not trouble me. Besides, matters were going well. In particular, the impenetrable undergrowth of music theory, harmony and the study of composition had been transformed into an accessible, attractive garden. I felt that the sudden flashes of insight and the musical sketches I made during my best hours no longer defied all the rules and laws, but that through assiduous study a narrow but clearly discernible path was leading to freedom. There were indeed hours and days and nights when I still seemed to be confronted by an insurmountable barrier and with a tired brain I struggled vainly against contradictions and pitfalls, but I did not despair again and I saw the narrow path become clearer and more accessible.

When school closed at the end of the term, the teacher who taught theory said to me, much to my surprise: "You are the only student this year who really seems to understand something about music. If you ever compose anything, I should like to see it."

With these comforting words ringing in my ears, I set off for my holidays. I had not been home for a long time, and during the railway journey I again pictured my native place with affection, and conjured up a series of half-forgotten memories of my childhood and early youth. My father was waiting for me at the station and we drove home in a cab. The following morning I already felt an urge to go for a walk through the old streets. For the first time I was overcome with a feeling of tragedy at my lost youthful fitness. It was painful to me to have to lean on a stick and limp with my crooked, stiff leg along these lanes, where every corner reminded me of boyish games and past pleasures. I came back home feeling dejected, and no matter whom I saw or whose voices I heard or what I thought about, everything reminded me bitterly of the past and my crippled state. At the same time, I was also unhappy because my mother was less enthusiastic than ever about my choice of career, although she did not actually tell me so. A musician who could make an appearance as a slender, erect virtuoso or an impressive-looking conductor, she might have conceded, but that a semicripple with only moderate qualifications and a shy disposition could bring himself to continue as a violinist was inconceivable to her. In this connection she was supported by an old friend who was a distant relative. My father had once forbidden her to come to the house, which caused her to conceive a violent dislike for him, although this did not keep her away, for she often came to see my mother while my father was at the office. She had never liked me and had scarcely ever spoken to me since I was a young boy. She saw in my choice of career an unfortunate sign of degeneration and in my accident an obvious punishment and the hand of Providence.

In order to give me pleasure, my father arranged for me to be invited to play a solo in a concert to be given by the town's Music Society. But I felt I could not do so. I refused and retired for many days to the small room which I had occupied as a boy. I was particularly harassed by all the questions I had to answer and by having to account for myself all the time, so that I hardly ever went out. I then found myself looking out of the window at the life in the street and at the school children, and above all I looked at the young girls with unhappy longing.

How could I ever hope to declare my love to a girl again, I thought! I should always have to stand outside, as at a dance, and look on, and never be taken seriously by girls, and if any were very friendly with me, it would be out of sympathy. Oh, I was more than sick of sympathy!

As it was, I could not remain at home. My parents also suffered considerably as a result of my extreme melancholy and scarcely raised any objection when I asked permission to set off immediately on the long-planned journey that my father had promised me. Throughout my life my infirmity made trouble for me and destroyed my heart's wishes and hopes, but I never felt my weakness and deformity so keenly as I did then, when the sight of every healthy young man and every pretty woman depressed and hurt me. I slowly grew used to my stick and to the limp until it hardly bothered me any more, so that with the passing of years I had to accustom myself to bearing the awareness of my injury without bitterness, but with resignation and humor.

Fortunately, I was able to travel alone and did not need to wait for anything. The thought of any companion would have been repugnant to me and would have disturbed my need for inner peace. I already felt better as I sat in the train and there was no one to look at me curiously and sympathetically. I traveled a day and night without stopping, with a feeling of really taking flight, and breathed a sigh of relief when, on the second day, I caught sight of high mountain peaks through steamed windows. I reached the last station as it was growing dark. I went wearily yet happily along dark lanes to the first inn of a compact little town. After a glass of deep red wine I slept for ten hours, throwing off the weariness of travel and also a good deal of the distress of mind with which I had come.

The following morning I took a seat in the small mountain train that traveled through narrow valleys and past white sparkling streams toward the mountains. Then, from a small, remote station, I traveled by coach; by middday I was in one of the highest villages in the country.

I stayed right into the autumn in the only small inn of the quiet little village, at times being the only guest. I had had it in mind to rest here for a short time and then travel farther through Switzerland and see some more of foreign parts and the world. But there was a wind at that height which blew air across that was so fresh and strong I felt I never wanted to leave it. One side of the steep valley was covered almost to the top with fir trees; the other slope was sheer rock. I spent my days here, by the sun-warmed rocks, or by the side of one of the swift, wild streams, the music of which could be heard during the night throughout the whole village. At the beginning I enjoyed the solitude like a cool, healing drink. No one bothered about me; no one showed any curiosity or sympathy toward me. I was alone and free like a bird in the air and I soon forgot my pain and unhealthy feelings of envy. At times I regretted being unable to go far into the mountains to see unknown valleys and peaks and to climb along dangerous paths. Yet I was not unhappy. After the events and excitement of the past months, the calm solitude surrounded me like a fortress. I found peace again and learned to accept my physical defect with resignation, although perhaps not with cheerfulness.

The weeks up there were almost the most beautiful in my life. I breathed the pure, clear air, drank the icy water from streams and watched the herds of goats grazing on the steep slopes, guarded by dark-haired, musing goatherds. At times I heard storms resound through the valley and saw mists and clouds at unusually close quarters. In the clefts of rocks I observed the small, delicate, bright colored flowers and the many wonderful mosses, and on clear days I used to like to walk uphill for an hour until I could see the clearly outlined distant peaks of high mountains, their blue silhouettes, and white, sparkling snow fields across the other side of the hill. On one part of the footpath where a thin trickle of water from a small spring kept it damp, I found on every fine day a swarm of hundreds of small, blue butterflies drinking the water. They scarcely moved when I approached, and if I disturbed them, they whirled about with a fluttering of tiny, silky wings. After I made the discovery, I only went that way on sunny days, and each time the dense, blue swarm was there, and each time it was a holiday.

When I consider it more closely, that period was not really as perfectly serene and sunny and joyous as it seems in retrospect. There were not only days when there was fog or rain, and even days when it snowed and was bitter cold; there were also days when it was stormy and inclement within me.

I was not used to being alone, and after the first days of repose and delight had passed, I again felt the pain from which I had run away return suddenly, at times with dreadful intensity. Many a cold evening I sat in my tiny room with my traveling rug over my knees, wearily and unrestrainedly giving way to foolish thoughts. Everything that young blood desired and hoped for, parties and the gaiety of dancing, the love of women and adventure, the triumph of strength and love, lay on another distant shore, far removed and inaccessible to me forever. Even that wild, defiant period of half-forced gaiety, which had ended in my toboggan accident, then seemed in my memory to be beautiful and colored in a paradisiacal way, like a lost land of pleasure, the echo of which still came across to me with bacchanal intoxication from the distance. And at times, when storms passed over at night, when the continual sound of the cold, down-pouring rain was drowned by the strong, plaintive rustling through the storm-swept fir wood, and when a thousand inexplicable sounds of a sleepless summer night echoed through the girders of the roof of the frail house, I lay dreaming hopelessly and restlessly about life and the tumult of love, raging and reproaching God. I felt like a miserable poet and dreamer whose most beautiful dream was only a thin, colored soap bubble, while thousands of others in the world, happy in their youthful strength, streched out joyous hands for all the prizes of life.

Just as I seemed to see all the glorious beauty of the mountains, and everything that my senses enjoyed, as through a veil and from a great distance, so also did there arise between me and the frequent wild outbursts of grief a veil and a slight feeling of strangeness, and soon the brightness of the days and the grief of the nights were like external voices which I could listen to with a heart free of pain. I saw and felt myself like a mass of moving clouds, like a battlefield full of fighting troops, whether I experienced pleasure and enjoyment, or grief and depression, both moods seemed clearer and more comprehensible to me. They freed themselves from my soul and approached me from the outside in the form of harmonies and a series of sounds that I heard as if in my sleep and that took possession of me against my will.

It was in the quiet of one evening when I was returning from the rocky side of the valley that I understood it all clearly for the first time, and as I meditated upon it and found myself to be a riddle, it suddenly occurred to me what it all signified — that it was the return of those strange remote hours of which I had a premonition-filled foretaste when I was younger. And with this memory, that wonderful clarity returned, the almost glasslike brightness and transparency of feelings where everything appeared without a mask, where things were no longer labeled sorrow or happiness, but everything signified strength and sound and creative release. Music was arising from the turmoil, iridescence and conflict of my awakened sensibilities.

I now viewed the bright days, the sunshine and the woods, the brown rocks and the distant snow-covered mountains with heightened feelings of happiness and joy, and with a new conception. During the dark hours I felt my sick heart expand and beat more furiously, and I no longer made any distinction between pleasure and pain, but one was similar to the other; both hurt and both were precious. Whether I felt pain or joy, my discovered strength stood peacefully outside looking on and knew that light and dark were closely related and that sorrow and peace were rhythm, part and spirit of the same great music.

I could not write this music down; it was still strange to me and its territory was unfamiliar. But I could hear it. I could feel the world in its perfection within me, and I could also retain something of it, a small part and echo of it, reduced and translated. I thought about it and concentrated on it for days. I found that it could be expressed with two violins and began in complete innocence, like a fledgling trying its wings, to write down my first sonata.

As I played the first movement on my violin in my room one morning, I was aware of its weakness, incompleteness and faults, but every bar went through me like a heart tremor. I did not know whether this music was good, but I knew that it was my own music, born and experienced within me and never heard anywhere else before.

Downstairs in the coffee room, motionless and with hair as white as snow, there sat year in year out the innkeeper's father, who was over eighty years old. He never said anything and only gazed around him attentively through peaceful-looking eyes. It was a mystery whether the solemn, silent man possessed more than human wisdom and stillness of spirit, or whether his mental powers had deserted him. I went down to that old man that morning, my violin under my arm, for I had observed that he always listened attentively to my playing and indeed to all music. As I found him alone, I stood before him, tuned my violin and played my first movement to him. The old man directed his peaceful-looking eyes, the whites of which were yellowish and the eyelids red, toward me and listened. Whenever I think of that music, I see the old man again, his immobile face and his serene eyes watching me. When I had finished, I nodded to him. He winked knowingly and seemed to understand everything. His yellowish eyes returned my glance; then he averted his gaze, lowered his head a little and returned to his former motionless state.

Autumn began early at that height, and as I made my departure one morning, there was a thick mist which fell in fine drops as cold rain, but I took with me the sunshine of the good days and also, as a thankful remembrance, courage for my next path in life.

Chapter Three

During my last term at the School of Music, I made the acquaintance of the singer Muoth, who had quite a creditable reputation in the town. He had finished his studies four years before and immediately obtained a position at the Opera House, where he was at present still taking lesser roles and, compared to older and better-liked singers, did not shine. Many people, however, considered him to be a future celebrity whose next step must lead him to fame. I had seen him on the stage in a number of roles and he had strongly impressed me, although not always favorably.

We became acquainted in the following

way. After my return to the School of Music, I took my violin sonata and two songs that I had composed to the teacher who had showed such kind sympathy toward me. He promised to look through the work and give me his opinion about it. It was a long time before he did so, and meantime I could detect a certain feeling of embarrassment on his part whenever I met him. Finally, he called me to his office one day and returned the manuscript to me.

"Here is your work," he said, visibly uncomfortable. "I hope you have not built too many hopes upon it. There is something in it, without any doubt, and you may yet achieve something. To be quite honest, I thought you were already more mature and tranquil. I did not really credit you with such a passionate nature. I expected something quieter and more pleasing, something more technically correct which could have been judged technically. But your work is not good technically, so I can say little about that. It is an audacious attempt, the merit of which I am unable to judge, but as your teacher I cannot praise it. You have put both less and more in it than I expected and thus place me in an embarrassing position. I am too much of a schoolmaster to overlook stylistic mistakes, and whether you will be able to outweigh them with originality, I should not like to say. I will therefore wait until I see more of your work. I wish you luck. You will go on composing in any event. That much I have noticed."

I then went away and did not know what to make of his verdict, which was no real criticism. It seemed to me that one should be able to look at a piece of work and see immediately whether it was done as a game and pastime, or whether it arose from necessity and the heart.

I put the manuscript away and decided to forget all about it for the time being and work really hard during my last few months of study.

One day I received an invitation from a family with strong musical interests. They were friends of my parents and I used to visit them once or twice a year. It was one of the usual evening gatherings except that there were one or two well-known people from the Opera House there whom I knew by sight. The singer Muoth was also there. He interested me most of all and it was the first time I had seen him at such close quarters. He was tall and handsome, a dark, imposing-looking man with a confident and perhaps already somewhat pampered manner. One could see that women liked him. Apart from his manner, he seemed neither pleased nor proud and there was something in his look and countenance that expressed much seeking and discontent. When I was introduced to him, he acknowledged me with a short stiff bow, without saying anything to me. After a while he suddenly came up to me and said: "Isn't your name Kuhn? Then I already know you a little. Professor S. has shown me your work. You must not hold it against him; he was not indiscreet. I came up just as he was looking at it, and as there was a song there, I looked at it with his permission."

I was surprised and embarrassed.

"Why are you telling me about it?" I asked. "I believe the professor didn't like it."

"Does that hurt you? Well, I liked the song very much. I could sing it if I had the accompaniment. I should like you to let me have it."

"You liked it? Can it be sung then?"

"Of course — although it would not be suitable for every kind of concert. I should like to have it for my own use at home."

"I will write it out for you. But why do you want to have it?"

"Because it interests me. There is real music in that song. You know it yourself."

He looked at me, and his way of looking made me feel uncomfortable: he looked me straight in the face, studying me with complete calmness, and his eyes were full of curiosity.

"You are younger than I thought. You must have already suffered a great deal."

"Yes," I said, "but I cannot talk about it."

"You don't need to. I won't ask you any questions."

His look disturbed me. After all, he was

quite a well-known man and I was still a student, so that although I did not at all like his way of asking questions, I could only defend myself weakly and timidly. He was not arrogant but somehow he inspired my sense of modesty and I could only put up a slight resistance, for I felt no real antagonism toward him. I had a feeling that he was unhappy and that he had an instinctive, powerful way of seizing on people as if he wanted to snatch something from them that would console him. His dark, searching eyes were as sad as they were bold and the expression on his face made him look much older than he really was.

Soon afterward, while his remarks were still occupying my thoughts, I saw him chatting politely and merrily to the host's daughter, who was listening to him with delight and gazed at him as if he were a creature out of a fairy tale.

I had lived such a lonely life since my accident that I thought about this meeting for many days, and it disturbed me. I was too unsure of myself not to stand in awe of this superior man, and too lonely and in need of someone not to be flattered by his approach. Finally, I thought he had forgotten me and his whims of that evening. Then, to my confusion, he visited me at my rooms.

It was on a December evening and it was already dark. The singer knocked at the door and came in as if there were nothing remarkable about his visit, and without any introduction and superficialities he immediately entered into conversation with me. I had to let him have the song, and as he saw my hired piano in the room, he wanted to sing it at once. I had to sit down and accompany him and so I heard my song sung properly for the first time. It was sad and moved me against my will, for he did not sing it at full singing strength but softly, as if to himself. The text, which I had read in a magazine the previous year and had copied, was as follows:

> *When the south wind blows*
> *The avalanche tumbles*
> *And death's dirge rumbles.*
> *Is that God's will?*

Through the lands of men
I wander alone,
Ungreeted and unknown.
Is that God's will?

Pain is my lot,
My heart is like lead.
I fear God is dead.
    — Shall I then live?

From the way he sang it, I could tell that he liked the song.

We were silent for a short time; then I asked him if he could point out any mistakes and suggest any corrections.

Muoth gave me one of his keen looks and shook his head.

"There is nothing to correct," he said. "I don't know whether the composition is good or not. I don't understand anything about that. There is experience and feeling in the song, and because I don't write poetry myself, or compose, I am glad when I find something that seems individual and that I want to sing."

"But the text is not mine," I exclaimed.

"Isn't it? Well, it doesn't matter; the text is of secondary importance. You must have experienced it, otherwise you could not have written the music."

I offered him the copy which I had had ready for some days. He took it, rolled it up and pushed it into his coat pocket.

"Come and visit me sometime, if you want," he said and gave me his hand. "I know you lead a quiet life. I don't want to disturb it, but now and then one is glad to look a good fellow in the face."

When he had gone, his last words and his smile remained with me. They were in keeping with the song he had sung and with everything that I knew of the man. The longer I pondered upon it, the clearer it became to me, and in the end I felt I understood this man. I understood why he had come to me, why he liked my song, why he almost presumptuously intruded upon me, and why he seemed half shy, half bold to me. He was unhappy, an inward pain gnawed at him, and his loneliness had become intolerable to him. This unhappy man had been proud and had tasted solitude.

He could no longer endure it; he was searching for people, for a kind look and a little understanding, and he was ready to sacrifice himself for them. That is what I thought at the time.

My feelings toward Heinrich Muoth were not clear. I sensed his desires and unhappiness, yet I feared he could be a cruel, ruthless man who might use and then discard me. I was too young and my experience of people too limited to understand and accept the fact that he almost revealed himself naked to people and, in doing so, hardly seemed to know any shame. Yet I also saw that here was a sensitive passionate man who was suffering and who was alone. Involuntarily, I remembered rumors I had heard about Muoth, vague, disjointed, students' talk, the exact details of which I had forgotten but the echo and pattern of which I had preserved in my memory. There were wild tales of women and adventure, and without remembering one of them, I seemed to recall something about bloodshed — the linking of his name to a story of suicide or murder.

When I conquered my shyness and asked one of my colleagues about it, the matter seemed less serious than I had thought. Muoth, it was said, had had a love affair with a young woman of good family, and the latter had, in fact, committed suicide two years ago, not that anyone ventured to speak of the singer's involvement in this affair in anything but cautious allusions. Evidently it was my own imagination, stirred by the encounter with this unique and faintly ominous person, that had created that aura of dread around him. All the same, he must have suffered over that love affair.

I did not have the courage to go to see him. I could not conceal the fact from myself that Heinrich Muoth was an unhappy and perhaps desperate person who wanted and needed me, and at times I felt I ought to obey the call and that I was contemptible not to do so. Yet I did not go. Another feeling prevented me: I could not give Muoth what he sought from me. I was quite different from him and even if in many ways I was also isolated and not fully understood by other people, even if I was different from everyone else and separated from most people by fate and my talents, I did not want to make an issue of it. Though the singer might be demonic in some ways, I definitely was not, and an inner necessity made me resist the spectacular and unusual. I had a feeling of aversion and repugnance toward Muoth's vehement manner. He was a man of the theater and an adventurer, I thought, and he was perhaps destined to live a tragic and public life. On the contrary, I wanted a quiet life; excitement and audacious talk did not suit me — resignation was my lot. That was how I argued with myself to set my mind at rest. A man had knocked at my door. I was sorry for him and perhaps I ought to put him before myself, but I wanted peace and did not want to let him in. I threw myself energetically into my work but could not rid myself of the tormenting idea that someone stood behind me and tugged at me.

As I did not come, Muoth again took the initiative. I received a note from him written in large bold characters, which read:

Dear Sir,

I usually celebrate my birthday on the 11th January with a few friends. Would you like to come along? It would give us pleasure if we could hear your new sonata on this occasion. What do you think? Have you a colleague with whom you could play it, or shall I send someone to you? Stefan Kranzl would be agreeable. It would please me very much.

HEINRICH MUOTH

I had not expected that — to play my music, which no one yet knew about, before experts, and to play the violin with Kranzl! Ashamed and grateful, I accepted the invitation, and only two days later I was requested by Kranzl to send him the music. After another two days, he invited me to visit him. The well-known violinist was still young. He was very pale and slender and looked like a virtuoso.

As soon as I entered, he said, "So you are Muoth's friend! Well, let us start straight away. If we pay attention, we'll have it after playing it two or three times."

Then he placed a stand before me, gave me the second-violin part, marked time and began with his light sensitive touch, so that in comparison I was quite feeble.

"Not so timidly!" he shouted across to me without stopping, and we played the music right through.

"That's all right!" he said. "It's a pity you haven't a better violin. But never mind. Now let us play the *allegro* a little faster, so that no one takes it for a funeral march. Ready!"

I then played my music quite confidently with the virtuoso, my modest violin sounding quite well alongside his valuable one. I was surprised to find this distinguished-looking man so natural, indeed, almost naive. As I began to feel more at home and gathered up courage, I asked him with some hesitation what he thought about my composition.

"You will have to ask someone else, my dear sir. I don't understand much about it. It's a little unusual, but people like that. If Muoth likes it, you can feel flattered. He is not easily pleased."

He gave me some advice regarding the playing and showed me a few places where alterations were necessary. We arranged to have another rehearsal the following day, and I then departed.

It was a comfort to me to find this man so natural and sincere. If he was one of Muoth's friends, perhaps I could also find a place among them. To be sure, he was an accomplished artist and I was a beginner without any great prospects. I was sorry that no one would give me an honest opinion of my work. The most severe criticism would have been preferable to these good-natured remarks which said nothing.

It was bitterly cold at that time — one even had difficulty keeping the rooms warm. My companions enthusiastically went skating. It was just a year since our outing with Liddy. That was not a happy period for me. I looked forward to the evening at Muoth's, not because I expected too much from it, but because I had had no friends or gaiety for so long. During the night before January 11, I was awakened by an unusual noise and an almost amazing feeling of warmth in the air. I rose and went to the window, surprised that it was no longer cold. The south wind had suddenly come. Damp and warm, it blew vigorously. High above, the storm swept the heavy masses of clouds across the sky; in the small gaps between the clouds a few stars, unusually large and brilliant, shone through. The roofs already had black patches on them, and in the morning, when I went out, all the snow was gone. The streets and people's faces seemed strangely altered, and everywhere there was a breath of premature spring.

That day I went about in a state of slightly feverish agitation, partly on account of the south wind and the intoxicating air, partly in anticipation of the evening. I frequently took out my sonata, played parts of it, then pushed it away again. Sometimes I found it quite beautiful and was proud and happy with it; at other times it seemed trivial, fragmented and vague to me. I could not have endured this state of agitation and anxiety much longer. In the end, I did not know whether I was looking forward to the forthcoming evening or not.

However, it came at last. I put on my overcoat, took my violin case with me, and went to find Muoth's house. It was with some difficulty that I found it in the dark. It was far out in the suburbs on an unknown and unfrequented road. The house stood by itself in a large garden, which looked untidy and neglected. From behind the unclosed gate a large dog sprang at me. Someone whistled it back from a window and, growling, it accompanied me to the entrance. A little old woman with an anxious expression on her face received me there, took my coat and led me along a brightly lit passage.

Kranzl, the violinist, lived in a very elegant fashion and I had expected Muoth, who was reputed to be rich, to live in a similarly lavish way. I now saw two large, spacious rooms, far too large for a bachelor who was seldom at home. Apart from that, everything was very simple, or not really simple but casual and unarranged. Part of the furniture was old and seemed to belong to the house, and there were new things bought indiscriminately and placed about the room without forethought. Only the lighting was splendid. There was no gas — instead, there were a large number of white candles in single, attractive pewter candlesticks. In the main room there was also a kind of chandelier, a plain brass circle containing many candles. Here the chief item of furniture was a very good grand piano.

In the room into which I was led, several men stood talking to each other. I put my violin case down and said: "Good evening!" Some of them nodded and then turned to each other again. I stood there feeling uncomfortable. Then Kranzl, who was among them and had not seen me immediately, came across to me, held out his hand, introduced me to his friends and said: "Here is our new violinist. — Have you brought your violin with you?" Then he called across to the next room: "Muoth, the young man with the sonata is here."

Heinrich Muoth then came in, greeted me very warmly and took me into the music room, which looked cheerful and festive. An attractive woman in a white dress, an actress from the Royal Theatre, handed me a glass of sherry. To my surprise, I observed that apart from her no other colleagues of the host had been invited. She was the only lady present.

As I had emptied my glass very quickly, partly through embarrassment, partly from an instinctive need to get warm after the damp, evening walk, she poured out another and ignored my protests. "Take it. It won't do you any harm. We do not eat until after the music. Have you brought your violin with you — and the sonata?"

I made reserved replies and felt embarrassed. I did not know what her relationship was to Muoth. She seemed to be the mistress of the house. She was very attractive. I subsequently noted that my new friend went about only with very beautiful women

Meantime, everyone came into the music room. Muoth put up a music stand. Everyone sat down and soon I was playing the music with Kranzl. I played mechanically; it seemed poor to me. Only now and then for fleeting moments, like flashes of lightning, was I conscious of the fact that I was playing here with Kranzl and that the evening I had so long waited for with trepidation was here, and that a small gathering of experts and discerning musicians were sitting there listening to my sonata. Only during the *rondo* did I become aware that Kranzl was playing magnificently, but I was still so shy and distracted from the music that I continually thought about other things and it suddenly occurred to me that I had not even congratulated Muoth on his birthday.

We finished playing the sonata. The pretty lady rose, held out her hand to Kranzl and me, and opened the door of a smaller room, where a table was set for a meal, with flowers and bottles of wine.

"At last!" cried one of the men. "I'm nearly starving."

"You're a shocking person," the lady replied. "What will the composer think?"

"Which composer? Is he here?"

She pointed me out. "There he is."

He looked at me and laughed. "You should have told me that before. Anyway, the music was very enjoyable. But when a man is hungry —"

We began the meal, and as soon as the soup was finished and the white wine was poured out, Kranzl rose and proposed a toast to the host on the occasion of his birthday. Immediately after the toast, Muoth rose to his feet. "My dear Kranzl, if you think I am going to make a speech in reply, you are mistaken. I don't want any more speeches, please. But perhaps the only one that is necessary I will take upon myself. I thank our young friend for his sonata, which I think is splendid. Perhaps our friend Kranzl will someday be glad to receive music of his to play, which he should do, for he played the sonata very sympathetically. I drink a toast to the composer and to our good friendship."

They all clinked glasses, laughed, chaffed me a little, and soon the good wine helped to produce an atmosphere of gaiety to which I gave in with relief. It was a long time since I had enjoyed myself and felt at ease in this way, and in fact I had not done so for a whole year. Now the laughter and wine, the clinking of glasses, the intermingling of voices and the sight of a gay, pretty woman opened up closed doors of pleasure to me, and I easily entered into the atmosphere of unrestrained merriment, of light and lively conversation and smiling faces.

Shortly after the meal, everyone rose and returned to the music room, where wine and cigarettes were handed round. A quiet-looking man who had not spoken much, and whose name I did not know, came up to me and said some kind words about the sonata, I have quite forgotten what. Then the actress drew me into conversation and Muoth sat down beside us. We drank another glass of wine to our friendship, and suddenly his dark, sad eyes sparkled and he said: "I know your story now." He turned to the lady. "He broke his bones while tobogganing, out of love for a pretty girl." Then he turned to me again. "That is beautiful — to go head over heels down the hill at the moment when love is at its peak and is quite unsullied. It is worth losing a healthy leg for that." Laughing, he emptied his glass and again looked gloomy and thoughtful. Then he said: "What made you interested in composing?"

I told him how music had affected me since I was a young boy. I told him about the previous summer, about my flight into the mountains, about the song and the sonata.

"I see," he said slowly, "but why does it give you pleasure? You can't express sorrow on paper and be finished with it."

"I don't want to do that," I replied. "I don't want to thrust aside and be rid of anything but weakness and constriction. I want to feel that pleasure and pain arise from the same source, that they are aspects of the same force and portions of the same piece of music, each beautiful and each essential."

"Man," he shouted vehemently, "you have a crippled leg! Can music make you forget it?"

"No, why? In any case, I can never make it better."

"And doesn't that make you despair?"

"It does not please me, you can be sure of that, but I hope it will never bring me to despair."

"Then you are lucky, but I wouldn't exchange a leg for that kind of luck. So that is how it is with your music! Marian, this is the magic of art that we read about so much in books."

"Don't talk like that!" I cried angrily. "You yourself don't sing just for your salary but because it is a source of pleasure and satisfaction to you. Why do you mock me and yourself? I think it is cruel."

"Hush," said Marian, "or Muoth will become angry."

He looked at me and said, "I won't be angry. You are quite right, really. But you can't feel so bad about your leg. Otherwise music-making would not be such a compensation to you. You are a contented sort of person. Anything can happen to you and you still remain contented — but I would never have believed it." Muoth sprang angrily to his feet. "And it isn't true. You set the Avalanche Song to music; that was no indication of consolation and satisfaction — but of despair. Listen!"

Suddenly he went to the piano and it became quieter in the room. He began to play, made a mistake, then omitted the introduction and sang the song. He now sang it differently from the way he had sung it in my room, and I could tell that he had sung it often since then. He now sang it aloud in the deep baritone voice that I had heard from the stage, and the strength and intense feeling in his voice made one forget the unrelieved distress of the song.

"This man says he wrote that purely for pleasure. He doesn't know anything about despair and is perfectly contented with his lot," he cried and pointed his finger at me. There were tears of shame and anger in my eyes. I saw everything through a mist, and in order to end it I stood up to go.

Then I felt a delicate yet strong hand press me back into the armchair and gently stroke my hair, so that tingling warm waves washed over me, I closed my eyes, and choked back my tears. Looking up, I saw Heinrich Muoth standing in front of me. The others did not appear to have observed the whole scene and my agitation. They were drinking wine and laughing.

"You are a child," said Muoth softly. "When a man writes songs like that, he should be above this kind of thing. But I am sorry. I find a person whom I like and we have hardly been together at all when I begin to pick a quarrel with him."

"Oh, all right," I said with embarrassment, "but I should like to go home now. The best part of the evening is finished."

"Very well, I will not press you to stay. The rest of us will have another drink yet, I think. Would you mind seeing Marian home? She lives on the inner side of the moat; it is not out of your way."

The pretty woman looked at him curiously for a moment. Then she turned to me and said, "Will you?" I said, "With pleasure," and stood up. We only said goodbye to Muoth. In the anteroom a hired servant helped us on with our coats; then the little old woman appeared sleepily and took us through the garden to the gate by the light of a large lantern. The wind was still warm and caressing; it drew along masses of black clouds and stirred the tops of the bare trees.

I did not venture to offer Marian my arm, but she took it unasked, breathed in the night air with her head thrown back and looked up at me inquiringly and trustfully. I still seemed to feel her soft hand on my hair. She walked slowly and seemed to want to lead me.

"There are cabs over there," I said, for it was painful to me that she should adapt herself to my lame walk and it made me suffer to have to limp beside this warm, healthy, slender woman.

"Let us walk a little," she said. She took care to walk very slowly, and if I had had my way I should have drawn her still closer to me. But I was filled with so much pain and anger that I released her arm, and when she looked at me with surprise, I said to her: "It is no good like this. Pardon me, I must walk alone." She walked anxiously and sympathetically by my side, and all that was needed for me to say and do the opposite of what I said and did was an upright walk and the awareness of physical well-being. I became quiet, as well as abrupt in my answers. I could not do otherwise or I should have had tears in my eyes and longed to feel her hand on my head again. I would have preferred to escape from her at the next side street. I did not want her to walk slowly, to show me consideration and pity me.

"Are you vexed with him?" she said at last.

"No, it was stupid of me. I hardly know him yet."

"He upsets me when he is like that. There are days when I am afraid of him."

"You, too?"

"Yes, more than anyone. He hurts no one more than himself. He hates himself at times."

"Oh, he puts on a pose."

"What did you say?" she said startled.

"He is an actor. What does he want to mock himself and others for? Why does he have to draw out the experiences and secrets from a friend and ridicule them — the miserable wretch!"

My previous anger found a way into my speech again. I wanted to insult and disparage this man who had hurt me and whom I really envied. Also my respect for the lady had decreased since she defended him and openly admitted it to me. Wasn't it bad enough that she had been the only woman at this bachelors' drinking party? I was used to little license in these things, and I was ashamed to have a yearning for this pretty woman at the same time. I preferred in my vexation to start a quarrel with her rather than feel her pity any longer. If she thought me rude and left me, it would be better than staying and being kind to me.

But she put her hand on my arm. "Stop," she cried warmly, so that her voice moved me despite myself. "Don't say any more! What is the matter with you? Muoth wounded you with two or three words because you were not skillful or courageous enough to defend yourself, and now that you have left, you attack him in hateful language in front of me. I ought to let you walk alone!"

"As you wish. I only said what I thought."

"Don't lie! You accepted his invitation and you played your music to him. You saw how he liked it, how it pleased you and cheered you up. And now, because you are angry and took offense at a few words he said, you begin to insult him. You shouldn't do that, and I will put it down to the wine you have had."

It appeared to me that she suddenly realized how things were with me and that it was not the wine that had excited me; she changed her tone, although I did not make the slightest attempt to vindicate myself. I was defenseless.

"You don't know Muoth yet," she

continued. "You have heard him sing, haven't you? That is what he is like, fierce and violent, but mostly against himself. He is an emotional man; he has great vigor but no goal. At every moment he would like to taste the whole world, and whatever he has and whatever he does only constitutes an infinitesimal part of it. He drinks and is never drunk; he has women and is never happy; he sings magnificently and yet does not want to be an artist. If he likes anyone, he hurts him. He pretends to despise all who are contented, but it is really hatred against himself because he does not know contentment. That is what he is like. And he has shown friendship toward you, as much as he is capable of doing."

I maintained an obstinate silence.

"Perhaps you don't need him," she began again. "You have other friends. But when we see someone suffer and be ill-mannered because of his suffering, we ought to be indulgent and forgive him."

Yes, I thought, one should do that. Gradually the walk in the night cooled me down, and although my own wound was still open and needed healing, I was induced to think more and more about what Marian had said and about my stupid behavior that evening. I felt that I was a miserable creature who really owed an apology. Now that the courage the wine had given me had worn off, I was seized by an unpleasantly sentimental mood against which I fought. I did not say much more to the pretty woman, who now seemed agitated and moody herself as she walked beside me along the dark streets where, here and there, the light of a lamp was suddenly reflected on the dark surface of the wet ground. It occurred to me that I had left my violin in Muoth's house; in the meantime I was again filled with astonishment and alarm at everything. The evening had turned out to be so different from what I had anticipated. Heinrich Muoth and Kranzl the violinist, and also the radiant Marian, who played the role of queen, had all climbed down from their pedestals. They were not gods or saints who dwelt on Olympian heights, but mere mortals;

one was small and droll, another was oppressed and conceited, Muoth was wretched and self-tormented, the charming woman was pathetic and miserable as the lady friend of a restless sensualist who knew no joy, and yet she was good and kind and acquainted with suffering. I, myself, felt changed. I was no longer a single person but a part of all people, seeing good and bad in all. I felt I could not love a person here and hate another person there. I was ashamed of my lack of understanding and saw clearly for the first time in my young life that one could not go through life and among people so simply, hating one person and loving another, respecting one person and despising another, but all these emotions were closely tied up, scarcely separable and at times scarcely distinguishable. I looked at the woman walking by my side who was now also silent as if she too realized that the nature of many things was different from what she had thought and said.

At last we reached her house. She held out her hand to me, which I gently pressed and kissed. "Sleep well!" she said kindly but without a smile.

I did, too. I went home and to bed, I know not how, fell asleep immediately and slept far into the next morning. Then I rose like the man in the jack-in-the-box, did my exercises, and washed and dressed myself. It was only when I saw my coat hanging on the chair and missed my violin case that I thought of the previous day. Meantime, I had slept well and felt better. I could not link up the thoughts I had had the previous night. There remained only small, strange, inward experiences in my memory and a feeling of surprise that I was still unchanged and the same as ever.

I wanted to work but my violin was not there. So I went out, at first irresolutely, then with determination, in the direction I had gone yesterday and arrived at Muoth's house. Even from the garden gate I heard him singing. The dog sprang at me and was led away with difficulty by the old woman who had quickly come out. She allowed me to go in. I told her I only wanted to fetch my violin and did not want to disturb the gentleman. My violin case was in the anteroom and my violin was in the case. My music had also been put there. Muoth must have done that; he had thought about me. He was singing aloud close by. I could hear him walking quietly up and down as if wearing slippers. At times he would strike keys on the piano. His voice sounded clear and bright, more controlled than I had ever heard it at the theater. He was practicing a role that was unknown to me. He repeated parts of it a number of times and walked quickly up and down the room.

I had taken my things and was going to leave. I felt quite calm and hardly affected by the memory of the previous day. But I was curious to see him and to know whether he had changed. I went nearer, and almost involuntarily I put my hand on the handle, turned it and stood in the open doorway.

Muoth turned round while singing. He was in a shirt, in a very long, fine, white shirt and looked fresh, as if he had just had a bath. Too late I took fright at having surprised him like that. However, he seemed neither surprised that I had come in without knocking nor embarrassed because he was not dressed. Just as if everything was perfectly normal, he held out his hand and asked: "Have you had breakfast yet?" Then, as I said yes, he sat down by the piano.

"Imagine, that's a part I'm supposed to *sing!* Just listen to this aria — what a mishmash! The opera is to be given at the Royal Opera House with Büttner and Duelli! But that doesn't interest you or me, really. How are you? Have you had a good rest? You didn't look so well when you left last night. And you were annoyed with me too. Anyway, we won't start that nonsense again now."

And straight away, without giving me a chance to say anything, he said: "You know, Kranzl is a bore. He won't play your sonata."

"But he played it yesterday."

"I mean at a concert. I wanted him to take it on, but he won't. It would have been grand if it had been included in, say, a matinee concert next winter.

Kranzl isn't a fool, you know, but he is lazy. He is always playing Russian music by an 'insky' or 'owsky.' He doesn't like learning anything new."

"I don't think," I began, "that the sonata is suitable for a concert and I never had that in mind. It is still not flawless technically."

"That's nonsense! You and your artistic pride! We're not like your schoolteachers and worse things will doubtless be played, particularly by Kranzl. But I have another idea. You must give me the song and write some more soon! I am leaving here in the spring. I have handed in my resignation and am going on a long holiday, during which I want to give one or two concerts, but with something new, not Schubert, Wolf, Löwe and the others we hear every evening. I want at least one or two new and unknown pieces of music, such as the Avalanche Song. What do you think?"

The prospect of my songs being sung in public by Muoth was like a gateway to the future through the bars of which I could see spendid vistas. For that very reason I wanted to be cautious and neither abuse Muoth's kindness nor bind myself to him too much. It seemed to me that he wanted to draw me to him somewhat too forcibly, to dazzle me and in some way overpower me. Therefore I hardly committed myself.

"I will see," I said. "You are very kind to me, I realize that, but I cannot promise anything. I am at the end of my studies and must now think about good testimonials. Whether I shall ever make my way as a composer is uncertain. Meantime, I am a violinist and must try to obtain a position soon."

"Oh, yes, you can do all that. But you may think of another song like that one, which you can let me have. Will you?"

"Yes, of course, although I don't know why you take such an interest in me."

"Are you afraid of me? I simply like your music. I should like to sing some more of your songs and look forward to doing so. It is pure egoism."

"All right, but why did you talk to me as you did yesterday?"

"Oh, you are still offended! What did I really say? I no longer remember. Anyway, I didn't intend to treat you roughly, as I seem to have done. But you can defend yourself! One talks, and every person is as he is and as he must be, and people have to accept each other."

"That's what I think, but you do just the opposite. You provoke me and do not accept what I say. You draw out of me things that I don't want to think about myself and that are my affair, and throw them back in my face like a reproach. You even mock me about my leg."

Heinrich Muoth said slowly: "Well, well, people are different. One man is wild if you tell him the truth, and another can't bear it if you spout platitudes. You were annoyed because I didn't treat you with false respect and I was annoyed because you were on the defensive and tried to delude me with fine phrases about the solace of art."

"I meant what I said, only I am not used to talking about these things. And I won't talk about the other matter either. How things seem to me, whether I am sad or in despair and how my leg came to be injured, I want to keep to myself, and I don't want to let anyone drag them out of me and mock me about them."

He stood up. "I haven't anything on yet. I'll go and get dressed. You're a good fellow. I'm not, I know. We won't talk about it so much again. Hasn't it occurred to you that I like you? Just wait a little. Sit down by the piano until I'm dressed. Do you sing? — No? — Well, I'll only be a few minutes."

He soon returned dressed from the adjoining room.

"We'll go into town now and have a meal," he said lightly. He did not ask whether it suited me. He said, "We'll go," and we went. For however much his manner annoyed me, it impressed me; he was the stronger character of the two. At the same time, he displayed a whimsical, childlike disposition in his conversation and behavior which was often charming and which quite won me over.

From that time I saw Muoth often. He frequently sent me tickets for the opera, sometimes invited me down to play the violin, and if I did not like everything about him, there were many things I could say to him without his taking offense. A friendship was established between us, at that time my only one, and I almost began to fear the time when he would no longer be there. He had in fact handed in his resignation and could not be pressed to stay, despite a number of requests and inducements. At times he hinted that there might be a part for him at a large theater in the autumn, but it was not yet arranged. In the meantime spring arrived.

One day I went to Muoth's house for the last gentlemen's gathering. We drank to our next meeting and the future, and this time there was no woman present. Muoth accompanied us to the garden gate early in the morning. He waved us farewell and returned shivering in the morning mist to his already half-emptied rooms, accompanied by the leaping and barking dog. It seemed to me that a section of my life and experience had now ended. I felt I knew Muoth well enough to be sure that he would soon forget us all. Only now did I see clearly and unmistakably how much I had liked this moody, imperious man.

The time for my departure had also arrived. I made my last visits to places and to people whom I would remember kindly. I also went once more up to the high road and looked down at the slope, which I would not indeed forget.

I set off home to an unknown and apparently uninteresting future. I had no situation and I could not give independent concerts. At home there only awaited me, to my dismay, some students who wanted violin lessons. To be sure, my parents also awaited me and they were rich enough to see that I did not want for anything, and were tactful and kind enough not to press me and ask what was to become of me. But right from the beginning I knew that I should not be able to endure it long.

There is not much for me to say about the ten months that I spent at home.

During this time I gave lessons to three students and despite everything was not really unhappy. People lived here also; things also happened here every day, but I only had a feeling of polite indifference toward everything. Nothing touched my heart, nothing swept me along. On the other hand, I secretly experienced strange, entrancing hours with music, when my whole way of life appeared petrified and estranged and only a hunger for music remained that often tormented me unbearably during the violin lessons and certainly made me a bad teacher. But afterwards, when I had fulfilled my obligations, or had evaded my lessons with cunning and excuses, I relapsed into a wonderful dreamlike state in which I built bold sound edifices, erected magnificent castles in the air, raised arches casting long shadows, and created musical patterns as light and delicate as soap bubbles.

While I went about in a state of stupefaction and absorption which drove away my previous companions and worried my parents, the dammed-up spring within me burst open even more forcibly and profusely than it had done the previous year in the mountains. The fruits of seemingly lost years, during which I had worked and dreamed, suddenly ripened and fell softly and gently, one after the other. They were sweet and fragrant; they surrounded me in almost overwhelming abundance and I picked them up with hesitation and mistrust. It began with a song, then a violin fantasia followed, then a string quartet, and when after a few months I had composed some more songs and several symphonic themes, I felt that it was all only the beginning and an attempt. Inwardly, I had visions of a great symphony; in my wildest moments I even thought of an opera. Meanwhile, from time to time I wrote polite letters to conductors and theaters, enclosed copies of testimonials from my teachers and humbly asked to be remembered for the next vacancy for a violinist. There came short, polite replies beginning "Dear Sir" and sometimes there were no replies, and there was no promise of an appointment. Then for a day or two I felt insignificant and retreated into myself, gave conscientious lessons and wrote more polite letters. Yet immediately afterwards I felt that my head was still full of music that I wanted to write down. Hardly had I begun composing again when the letters, theaters, orchestras, conductors and "Dear Sirs" faded out of my thoughts and I found myself fully occupied and contented.

But these are memories that one cannot properly describe, like most recollections. What a person really is and experiences, how he develops and matures, grows feeble and dies, is all indescribable. The lives of ordinary working people can be boring, but the activities and destinies of idlers are interesting. However rich that period remains in my memory, I cannot say anything about it, for I remained apart from ordinary social life. Only once, for moments, did I again come closer to a person whom I will not forget. He was a teacher called Lohe.

One day, late in the autumn, I went for

a walk. A modest villa suburb had arisen on the south side of the town. No rich people dwelt in the small, inexpensive houses with their neat gardens, but respectable middle class families and people who lived on small incomes. A clever young architect had erected a number of attractive houses here which I was interested to see.

It was a warm afternoon. Here and there, nuts had fallen belatedly from the trees; the small new houses and gardens were clearly outlined in the sunshine. They were of a simple design that appealed to me. I looked at them with the superficial interest that young people have in these things, when thoughts of house, home and family, rest days and holidays are still remote. The peaceful streets with their gardens made a very pleasing impression on me. I strolled along slowly, and as I was walking, I happened to read the names of the occupants on small bright plates on the garden gates.

The name "Konrad Lohe" was on one of these brass plates and, as I read it, it seemed familiar to me. I stood still and reflected. Then I remembered that that was the name of one of the teachers at the Grammar School. For a few moments the past rose before me, confronted me with surprise, and a mass of faces, teachers and friends, memories of nicknames and stories danced before me in fleeting waves. As I stood there looking at the brass plate, a man rose from behind a nearby currant bush where he had been bending down at work. He came forward and looked at me.

"Did you want me?" he asked, and it was Lohe, the teacher whom we used to call Lohengrin.

"Not really," I said and raised my hat. "I did not know that you lived here. I used to be one of your students."

He looked at me more keenly, observed my stick, reflected a moment and then pronounced my name. He had remembered not my face but my stiff leg, for he naturally knew about my accident. Then he asked me to come in.

His shirt sleeves were rolled up and he

was wearing a green gardening apron. He did not seem to have grown older and looked wonderfully well. We walked through the small, neat garden, then he led me to an open veranda, where we sat down.

"Well, I would never have recognized you," he said candidly. "I hope your memory of me has been a kind one."

"Not entirely," I said laughing. "You once punished me for something I did not do and declared my protestations of innocence to be lies. It was in the fourth grade."

He looked up with a troubled expression on his face. "You must not hold it against me. I am very sorry. With all the good intentions in the world, it continually happens with teachers that something goes wrong and an act of injustice is committed. I know of worse cases. That is one of the reasons why I left."

"Oh, aren't you still teaching?"

"Not for a long time now. I became ill, and when I recovered, my views had changed so much that I resigned. I tried to be a good teacher, but I wasn't one; you have to be born to it. So I gave it up and since then I have felt better."

I could see that. I inquired further, but he wanted to hear my story, which was soon told. He was not altogether pleased that I had become a musician. On the other hand, he showed great tact by his sympathy for my ill-fortune so that for once I was not offended. He discreetly tried to discover how I had succeeded in finding consolation, and was not satisfied with my half-evasive answers. With mysterious gesticulations, he intimated hesitatingly and yet impatiently, with much bashful circumlocution, that he knew of a solace, of complete wisdom which was there for every earnest seeker.

"I know," I said. "You mean the Bible."

Mr. Lohe smiled mysteriously. "The Bible is good. It is the way to knowledge, but it is not knowledge itself."

"Well, where is knowledge itself?"

"You will find it easily if you wish to. I will give you something to read that gives the principles of it. Have you heard of the study of Karma?"

"Karma? No, what is it?"

"You will find out. Just wait a minute!" He went away and was absent for a short time while I sat there surprised, not knowing what to expect, and looked down the garden where diminutive fruit trees stood in faultless rows. After a short time, Lohe returned. He looked at me, with his face beaming, and handed me a small book, which bore, in the middle of a mysterious symbolic pattern, the title *Theosophical Catechism for Beginners.*

"Take that with you," he said. "You may keep it, and if you want to study further, I can lend you some more books. This one is only an introduction. I owe everything to these teachings. I have become well in body and soul through them and hope they will do the same for you."

I took the small book and put it in my pocket. The man accompanied me through the garden down to the road, took friendly leave of me and asked me to come again soon. I looked at his face, which was good and happy, and it seemed to me that there could be no harm in trying the path to such happiness. So I went home with the little book in my pocket, curious about the first steps along this path to bliss.

Yet I only embarked upon it after a few days. On my return home, the call of music was again powerful. I threw myself into it and lived in a world of music. I wrote and played until the storm within me was again silenced and I could return calmly to everyday life. Then I immediately felt the need to study the new teachings, and sat holding in front of me the little book which I thought I could soon absorb.

But I did not find it so easy. The little book became massive in my hands and finally seemed unfathomable. It began with an interesting introduction on the many paths to wisdom to which everyone has access, and the theosophical brotherhood that stands independently for knowledge and inner perfection, in which every faith is respected and every path to the light is welcome. Then followed a cosmology that I did not understand, a division of the world into different "planes," and history into remarkable ages unknown to me, in which the lost continent of Atlantis was also included. I left this for a time and turned to the other chapters, where the doctrine of reincarnation was presented, which I understood better. Yet it was not quite clear to me whether it was all mythology and poetic fables, or whether it was to be taken literally. It seemed to me to be the latter, which I could not accept.

Then came the teachings about Karma. It appeared to me to be a religious interpretation of the law of causality, which was not unattractive to me. And so on. I soon realized that these teachings could only be of solace and value to those who could accept them literally, and sincerely believe them to be true. If, as it seemed to me, they were partly beautiful literature, partly intricate symbols, an attempt at a mythological explanation of the world, one could be instructed by them and hold them in esteem, but one could not learn how to live and gain strength from them. One could perhaps be a worthy and religious theosophist, but the final solace beckoned only to those who accepted simple beliefs without too much questioning. In the meantime, it was not for me.

All the same, I went to see the teacher several more times. Twelve years ago we had plagued each other with Greek and now, in quite a different way and equally unsuccessfully, he tried to be my teacher and guide. We did not become close friends, but I liked going to see him and for a time he was the only person with whom I discussed important aspects of my life. I did indeed realize that all this talk was of no value and at its best only led to clever phrases. Yet I found him soothing and worthy of reverence, this devout man who had coolly renounced church and knowledge and who in the latter half of his life experienced the peace and glory of religion through his naive belief in remarkable, subtly reasoned teachings.

Despite all my efforts, this path has always been closed to me. Yet I have a great leaning, which is not reciprocated, toward religious people who are fortified by and gain peace from one faith or another.

Chapter Four

During the short period of my visits to the pious theosophist and fruit grower, I one day received a small check, the reason for which was a mystery to me. It had been sent to me by a well-known north German concert agent with whom, however, I had never had any dealings. On making inquiries, I received the reply that this amount had been forwarded to me by order of Mr. Heinrich Muoth. He had sung at six concerts a song composed by me and this sum represented my fee.

I then wrote to Muoth, thanked him and asked for news. Above all, I wanted to know how my song had been received at the concerts. I had heard about

Muoth's recitals and had seen reviews of them once or twice in the newspapers, without however seeing my song mentioned. I wrote to him about my activities and work in minute detail, as solitary people often do, and also enclosed one of my new songs. Then I waited for an answer. As I had still received none after four weeks, I forgot all about the whole matter again. Almost every day I wrote music, which haunted me as in a dream. During the intervals, however, I felt limp and discontented. I very much disliked giving lessons and felt I could not endure it much longer.

I therefore felt that a curse was lifted from me when I finally received a letter from Muoth. He wrote:

Dear Mr. Kuhn,
I am no letter writer. I did not answer your letter, as I did not really know what to say. But now I can put forward concrete proposals. I am now engaged at the Opera House here in R. and I should be pleased if you could also come here. You could, in the first

place, obtain a position here as a second violinist. The conductor is an intelligent, frank man, even though somewhat abrupt. You would probably also soon have an opportunity to play some of your music. We have good chamber concerts here. I also have something to tell you about your songs; one thing is that there is a publisher who wants to bring them out. But writing is such a bore. It would be better if you came. Come quickly and wire me about the position.

Yours,
MUOTH

I was thus suddenly dragged away from my unprofitable hermit's existence. I was again drawn into the stream of life, had hopes and cares, sorrows and joys. There was nothing to keep me, and my parents were glad to see me take my first definite step in my career in life. I sent a wire without delay, and three days later I was in R. with Muoth.

I had obtained accommodation in a hotel. I went to visit Muoth but did not find him in. Then he came to my hotel and unexpectedly stood before me. He held out his hand, asked me no questions, did not tell me anything and did not share my excitement in the slightest. He was used to letting himself be drawn along by events, only experiencing and taking seriously the present moment. He hardly gave me time to change my clothes and then took me to see Rössler, the conductor.

"This is Mr. Kuhn," he said.

Rössler nodded. "How do you do! What can I do for you?"

"He is the violinist," cried Muoth.

The conductor looked at me with surprise, turned to the singer again and said rudely: "You didn't tell me that the gentleman was lame. I must have people with straight limbs."

The blood rose to my face but Muoth remained calm. He just laughed. "Do you want him to dance, Rössler? I thought he was to play the violin. If he can't do that, we must send him away again. But let us hear him first."

"Very well, gentlemen. Mr. Kuhn,

come and see me tomorrow morning about nine o'clock, here in my rooms. Are you annoyed at what I said about the foot? Well, Muoth should have told me about it. Anyway, we shall see. Till tomorrow!"

As we went away, I reproached Muoth about it. He shrugged his shoulders and said that if he had mentioned my infirmity at the beginning, it would have been difficult to obtain the conductor's consent. Now I was here and if Rössler found me reasonably satisfactory, I would soon get to know the better side of his nature.

"But how could you recommend me in any case?" I asked. "You don't even know if I am any good."

"That's your affair. I thought you would be all right — and you will be too. You're such an unassuming fellow that if someone didn't give you a push at times, you would never get anywhere. That was a push — now you go ahead! You need not be afraid. Your predecessor wasn't much good."

We spent the evening in his rooms.

Here again he had rented some rooms in a remote district where there was a large garden and it was quiet. His powerful dog sprang forward to greet him. We had hardly sat down and warmed ourselves when the bell was rung and a tall, very beautiful woman came in and kept us company. It was the same atmosphere as previously, and his mistress was again a splendid aristocratic person. He seemed to take lovely women very much for granted and I looked at this latest lady love with sympathy and with the embarrassment that I always felt in the presence of attractive women. It was indeed not without envy, for with my lame leg it seemed to me I was unloved and without hope of love.

As in the past, we enjoyed ourselves and drank a great deal at Muoth's. He dominated us with his extreme but moody gaiety, which nevertheless charmed us. He sang for us enchantingly and also sang one of my songs. The three of us became very friendly; a feeling of warmth spread among us and drew us close. We were natural with each other and remained close as long as the warmth in us endured. The tall lady, who was called Lottie, was friendly toward me in a gentle way. It was not the first time that a beautiful and affectionate woman had treated me in this sympathetic and extremely confiding way. It hurt me this time too, but I now recognized this recurrent form of behavior and did not take it too much to heart. Sometimes I have even known women who have shown special friendship toward me. They all regarded me as incapable of jealousy as of love. In addition, there was that insufferable pity they had for me which evinced itself in an almost maternal trust.

Unfortunately, I still had no experience of such affairs and could not look on the happiness of love at close quarters without thinking about myself a little and feeling that I should also have liked to indulge in something similar. It spoiled my pleasure to some extent, but on the whole it was a pleasant evening in the company of this generous and beautiful woman and the fiery, vigorous and temperamental man who liked me and took an interest in me and yet could not show his affection in any different way than he did with women, namely in a forceful and moody fashion.

As we clinked glasses for the last time before I left, he nodded to me and said: "I really ought to drink to our good friendship, shouldn't I? I should certainly like to do so. But never mind, it will be all right just the same. At one time, whenever I met anyone I liked, I always addressed him immediately in an intimate fashion, but it isn't a good thing, least of all among colleagues. I quarreled with them just the same."

This time I did not have the bittersweet pleasure of having to accompany my friend's lady love home. She remained there and it was better so. The journey, the visit to the conductor, the suspense about the following morning and the renewed association with Muoth had all done me good. Only now did I see how forgotten, ill at ease and remote from people I had become during my long, lonely year of waiting, and with a sense of enjoyment and healthy anticipation, I was again alert and active among people, again belonging to the world.

The next morning I reported to Rössler in good time. I found him in his dressing gown and with his hair uncombed, but he made me welcome and, in a friendlier fashion than the previous day, he invited me to play the violin, placed handwritten music before me and sat down by the piano. I played as well as I could, but reading the badly written music gave me some trouble. When we had finished, he silently placed another sheet before me to play without any accompaniment, and then a third sheet.

"That's all right," he said. "You will have to become more used to reading the music; you're sometimes a little slow on the uptake. Come to the theater tonight. I will make room for you; then you can play your part next to the substitute who has filled the gap in the meantime. It will go a little hard at the beginning. Study the music well in advance. There is no rehearsal today. I will give you a note; take it to the theater at eleven o'clock and fetch the music."

I was not quite certain of my position but realized that this man did not like questions and I went away. At the theater no one wanted to know anything about the music or to listen to me. I was unused to the machinery there and was disconcerted. I sent a special messenger to Muoth. He came and immediately everything went smoothly. In the evening I played for the first time at the theater and was closely observed by the conductor. The following day I obtained the appointment.

So strange is a human being that in the midst of my new life and fulfilled wishes I was sometimes seized by a sudden, fleeting, almost subconscious desire for solitude, for even boring and empty days. It then seemed to me that the time I had spent at home and the dreary uneventful life from which I was so glad to escape were something desirable. In particular, I thought with real longing about the weeks I had spent in the mountains two years ago. I felt that I was not destined for well-being and happiness but for weakness and failure, and that without these shadows and sacrifices, the creative spring within me would flow more feebly and turbidly. At first there really was no question of quiet hours and creative work, and although I was living a full life, I continually thought I heard the dammed-up spring within me whisper softly and complainingly.

I enjoyed playing the violin in the orchestra. I poured over full scores a great deal and felt my way gradually in this field. Slowly I learned what I had only known theoretically and remotely, namely to understand the nature, color and significance of single instruments from the bottom upwards. At the same time, I studied ballet music and looked forward with greater earnestness to the time when I could venture to write an opera myself.

My close relationship with Muoth, who held one of the best positions at the Opera House, facilitated my progress and was quite useful to me. I was very sorry, however, that this had the opposite effect on my relationship with my colleagues. I did not make any close friends among the members of the orchestra, something I was only too willing to do. Only a first violinist, a Styrian called Teiser, took an interest in me and became my friend. He was ten years older than I, an honest, straightforward man with a gentle, delicate face that easily reddened. He was an extraordinarily accomplished musician and had a particularly keen and sensitive ear. He was one of those people who find satisfaction in their art without wanting to play any outstanding part. He was no virtuoso and had never composed anything. He was content to play the violin and derived his greatest pleasure from a thorough knowledge of technique. He knew every overture in detail, and knew as well as any conductor where delicacy and brilliant playing were necessary and where the introduction of another instrument produced a beautiful and original effect. This made him radiant and he enjoyed himself more than anyone else in the whole theater. He could play nearly all the instruments, so that I could ask him questions and learn from him daily.

For many months we discussed nothing but technique, but I liked him and he saw that I was anxious to learn. An unspoken understanding arose between us that did not fall far short of friendship. Then I finally told him about my violin sonata and asked him to play it with me sometime. He kindly agreed and came to my rooms at the appointed time. In order to please him, I obtained some wine from his native town. We drank a glass of the wine; then I put up the music and we began. He read the music very well, but suddenly he stopped and lowered his bow.

"I say, Kuhn," he said, "this really is lovely music and I don't want to play it just anyhow. I want to take it home and practice it first. May I?"

"Yes," I said, and when he came again, we played the sonata through twice. When we had finished, he slapped me on the shoulder and cried: "You modest creature! You pretend to be such an innocent and secretly you do things like this! I won't say much — I am not a professor, but it is beautiful!"

That was the first time that someone in whom I really had confidence had praised my work. I showed him all my music, including the songs that were just being published and were soon to appear. But I did not dare tell him that I was so bold as to think of composing an opera.

During those good days I was shocked by a small incident that I can never forget. At Muoth's, where I was a frequent visitor, I had not seen the pretty woman called Lottie for some time, but I did not think much about it because I did not want to become involved in any of his love affairs. I preferred not to know about them. I therefore did not inquire about her. Besides, he never talked to me about these things.

One afternoon I sat in my room studying a score. By the window, my black cat lay sleeping in the sunshine. The whole house was quiet. Then I heard someone enter by the front door who was stopped and questioned by the landlady, and then came and knocked at my door. I went to open it and a tall, elegant woman with a veil over her face entered and closed the door behind her. She took a few steps into the room, breathed deeply and then took off her veil. It was Lottie. She looked excited and I immediately guessed why she had come. At my request she sat down. She had shaken my hand but had not yet said anything. She seemed more at ease when she observed my embarrassment, as if she feared I might send her away immediately.

"Is it about Heinrich Muoth?" I asked at last.

She nodded. "Did he tell you anything?"

"No, I don't know anything. It is only what I thought."

She looked me in the face the way a sick person looks at a doctor, was silent and slowly took off her gloves. Suddenly she stood up, placed both hands on my shoulders and gazed at me with her big eyes.

"What shall I do? He is never at home, he never writes to me, he never even opens my letters! I have not been able to speak to him for three weeks. I went there yesterday. I know he was in but he did not open the door. He did not even whistle at his dog, who had torn my dress. He doesn't want to recognize me any more."

"Have you had a quarrel with him?" I asked only so that I should not remain silent.

She laughed. "Quarrel? Oh, we have had enough quarrels right from the beginning! I was used to that. No, he has even been polite to me lately, which I immediately mistrusted. On one occasion he wasn't there when he asked me to come; another time he said he was coming to see me and did not turn up. Finally, he began to address me formally. I would have preferred him to beat me again."

I was stunned. "Beat you!"

She laughed again. "Didn't you know? Oh, he has often beaten me, but not for a long time now. He has become polite;

he addresses me formally and does not want to know me any more. I expect he has someone else. That is why I have come here. Tell me, please! Has he another woman? You know, you must know!"

Before I could prevent it, she took hold of both my hands. I was astounded at what she had told me, but because I did not wish to discuss it and desired to end the scene I was almost glad that she did not give me a chance to speak, for I would not have known what to say.

Alternately hopeful and sorrowful, she was contented that I should listen to her. She asked me questions, told me things and burst into fits of weeping. All the time I looked at her pretty, tearful face and could think of nothing else except, "He has beaten her!" I seemed to see his clenched hand, and I shuddered at the thought of him, and of her too, who, having been beaten, scorned and repulsed, seemed to have no other thought and wish but to return to him and the same humiliations.

At last the flood subsided. Lottie

began to speak more slowly. She seemed embarrassed and conscious of the situation, became silent, and at the same time released my hands.

"There is no one else," I said gently, "at least not as far as I am aware."

She looked at me gratefully.

"But I can't help you," I continued. "I never talk to him about such things."

We were both silent awhile. I could not help but think of Marian, of pretty Marian, and that evening when we had walked arm-in-arm the same night the south wind had come, and how she had so loyally defended her lover. Had he beaten her also? And did she still pursue him?

"Why did you come to me?" I asked.

"I don't know. I had to do something. Do you know if he still thinks about me? You are a good man. You will help me, won't you? You could ask him sometime, speak about me . . ."

"No, I can't do that. If he still loves you, he will come to you himself. If not, then . . ."

"Then what?"

"Then let him go. He is not worthy that you should humble yourself so much."

Thereupon she smiled. "Oh, what do you know about love!"

She was right, I thought, but it hurt me just the same. If love did not come to me, if I stood outside, how could I be taken into anyone's confidence and be of help? I felt sorry for this woman but I despised her even more. If that was love, with cruelty here and humiliation there, then it was better to live without love.

"I don't want to argue," I said coolly. "I don't understand this kind of love."

Lottie fastened on her veil. "Very well, I'm going."

Then I felt sorry for her, but I did not want this ridiculous scene to be repeated, so I did not say anything. She walked toward the door and I opened it for her. I accompanied her past the inquisitive landlady to the stairs; then I bowed and she went away without saying anything more and without looking at me.

I looked after her sadly and could not rid myself of the memory of her for a long time. Was I really quite different from all these other people, from Marian, Lottie and Muoth? Was that really love? I saw all these passionate people reel about and drift haphazardly as if driven by a storm, the man filled with desire today, satiated on the morrow, loving fiercely and discarding brutally, sure of no affection and happy in no love; then there were the women who were infatuated with him, suffering insults and beatings, finally rejected and yet still clinging to him, degraded by jealousy and despised love, but still remaining faithful, like dogs. That day, for the first time in a very long while, I wept. I shed involuntary tears of vexation for these people, for my friend Muoth, and life and love, and also secret tears for myself who lived among everything as if on another planet, who did not understand life, who longed for love, yet was afraid of it.

I did not go to see Heinrich any more for a long time. He was enjoying triumphs as a Wagnerian singer and was beginning to be regarded as a star. I also had a moderate amount of publicity. My songs had been published and well received and two pieces of my chamber music had been performed. It was just a little encouraging recognition among friends; the critics still said little or were for the most part indulgent toward me as a beginner.

I spent a great deal of time with Teiser, the violinist. He liked me, praised my work, and took friendly pleasure in it. He prophesied great things for me and was always ready to play music with me. Just the same I felt that something was lacking. I was drawn to Muoth, although I still avoided him. I did not hear any more from Lottie. Why then was I not content? I reproached myself for not being satisfied with the company of Teiser, who was so good and loyal. But I found something lacking in him too. He was too happy, too cheerful, too contented; he seemed to have no depth. He did not speak well of Muoth. Sometimes when Muoth sang at the theater he looked at me and whispered: "He has faked it again! That man is quite spoiled. He doesn't sing Mozart and he knows why." I had to agree with him and yet I did so unwillingly. I was drawn to Muoth, but did not like to defend him. Muoth had something that Teiser did not have or understand and which bound me to him, and that was a continual desire, yearning and dissatisfaction. These same qualities drove me to study and work, to seize people to myself who always slipped away from me again, just as they eluded Muoth, who was goaded and tormented by the same dissatisfaction, though differently than I. I would always write music. I knew that. But I also wanted to create something but of happiness and abundance and uninterrupted joy, instead of continual longing and a sense of lack. Why was I not happy with what I had — my music? And why was Muoth not happy with what he possessed — his tremendous vitality and his women?

Teiser was lucky; he was not tormented by any desires for the unattainable. He derived a keen, unfailing pleasure from his art. He did not ask for more than it gave him, and outside his art he was even more easy to satisfy; he only needed a few friendly people, an occasional good glass of wine, and on free days an excursion into the country, for he liked walking and open-air life. If there was anything in the teachings of the theosophists, then this man was almost perfect; his disposition was so kind and he harbored so little passion and discontent. Yet even if I perhaps deceived myself, I did not wish to be like him. I did not want to be like anyone else. I wanted to remain in my own skin, although it was often so constrictive. I began to feel power within me as my work began to have some effect, and I was on the point of becoming proud. I had to find some kind of bridge to reach people, had to learn to live with them without always being the weaker. If there was no other way, perhaps my music would create a bridge. If people did not like me, they would have to like my music.

I could not rid myself of such foolish thoughts and yet I was ready to devote and sacrifice myself to someone who wanted me, to someone who really understood me. Was not music the secret law of the world? Did not the earth and stars move in a harmonious circle? And should I have to remain alone and not find people whose natures harmonized well with my own?

A year had gone by since I had been in this town. Apart for Muoth, Teiser and our conductor, Rössler, I had had few acquaintances at the beginning. Lately, however, I moved about in a larger circle, which did not particularly please or displease me. Since the performance of my chamber music, I had become acquainted with musicians in the town, outside the theater, and now enjoyed the easy and pleasant burden of a gently burgeoning reputation. I noticed that people knew and observed me. Of all fame, the sweetest is that which is not yet for any great success, which cannot cause envy and which does not isolate you. You go about with the feeling that here and there you are noticed, your name is known and you are praised; you meet people who welcome you with a smile, and acquaintances who give you a friendly nod. Younger people greet you with respect, and you secretly feel that the best is still to come, as all young people do, until they see that the best already lies behind them. My pleasure was diminished primarily by the feeling that there was always a touch of pity behind this recognition. Quite often I even felt that people were so kind and friendly toward me because I was a poor fellow and a cripple whom they wanted to console.

After a concert at which a violin duet of mine had been played, I made the acquaintance of a rich merchant called Imthor, who was reputed to be a lover of music and a patron of young talent. He was a rather small, quiet man with graying hair in whom one could detect neither his riches nor his love of art. But from what he said to me, I could see that he understood a geat deal about music; he did not give extravagant praise but quiet competent judgment, which was worth more. He told me what I had already known for a long time from other sources, namely, that many musical evenings were held at his house, and new as well as classical music was performed. He invited me to come and, before parting, said: "We have your songs at home and we like them. My daughter will also be glad if you will come."

Even before I had the chance to visit him he sent me a written invitation. Mr. Imthor asked permission for my trio in E flat major to be performed at his house. A violinist and a cellist, competent amateurs, were available, and the first violin part would be kept for me if I wished to play it. I knew that Imthor always paid a very good fee to professional musicians who played at his house. I would not like to accept this, yet did not know how to refuse the invitation. Finally, I accepted. The two other musicians came to see me, received their parts and we had a number of rehearsals. In the meantime, I called round to see Imthor, but found no one at home. Then the appointed evening arrived.

Imthor was a widower. He lived in an old, stately, middle-class house, one of the few still surrounded by its old garden, which had remained intact in the midst of the growing town. I saw little of the garden when I arrived in the evening, only a short drive with tall plane trees; in the lamplight one could see the light marks on their trunks. In between them were several old statues that had become darkened with age. Behind the tall trees the old, broad, low house stood unassumingly. From the front door, along the passages, stairs, and in all the rooms we passed through, the walls were closely covered with old pictures of family groups, faded landscapes, old-fashioned scenes and animals. I arrived at the same time as other guests. We were received by a housekeeper and taken inside.

There were not very many guests, but they seemed to fill the smallish rooms until the doors of the music room were opened. This was a large room and everything here looked new, the grand piano, the music cabinets, the lamps and the chairs; only the pictures on the walls were old here, too.

The other two musicians were already there. We put up the music stands, attended to the lighting, and began to tune up. Then a door was opened from the far end of the room, and a lady in a light dress came across the half-illumined room. The other two gentlemen greeted her respectfully. She was Imthor's daughter. She looked at me questioningly, then before we were introduced, she held out her hand to me and said: "I know you already. You are Mr. Kuhn, aren't you? I am Gertrude Imthor. You are very welcome."

The pretty girl had made an impression on me as soon as she had come in. Now her voice sounded so bright and kind that I pressed the outstretched hand warmly and looked with pleasure at the girl who had greeted me in such a charming, friendly manner.

"I'm looking forward to your trio," she said smiling, as though she had anticipated that I would be the way I was, and was now satisfied.

"I am, too," I said, not knowing what I was saying. I looked at her again and she nodded. Then she moved away, went out of the room, and my eyes followed her. She soon returned on her father's arm, and behind them came the guests. We three musicians were in our places ready to begin. Everyone sat down. A number of acquaintances nodded to me, the host shook hands with me, and when everyone had settled down, the electric lights were switched off, and only the large candles remained to light our music.

I had almost forgotten about my music. I looked for Gertrude at the back of the room. She sat leaning against a bookcase in the dim light. Her dark brown hair looked almost black. I could not see her eyes. Then I softly beat time, nodded, and we commenced the *andante* with a broad sweep of the bow.

Now that I was playing, I felt happy and at peace. I swayed gently to the rhythm and felt completely at ease with the music, which all seemed quite new to me, as if it had just been composed. My thoughts about the music and Gertrude Imthor flowed together clearly without a break. I drew my bow and gave directions with my glance. The music proceeded smoothly and steadily; it carried me with it along a golden path to Gertrude, whom I could no longer see and now no longer even desired to see. I dedicated my music and my life's breath, my thoughts and my heart to her, as an early-morning wanderer surrenders himself to the blue sky and the bright dew on the meadows, involuntarily and without losing himself. Simultaneous with this feeling of well-being and the increasing volume of sound, I was overwhelmed by an astonishing feeling of happiness, for I suddenly knew what love was. It was not a new feeling, but a clarification and confirmation of old premonitions, a return to a native country.

The first movement was finished; there was pause for a few moments.

Then there were the slightly discordant sounds of instruments being tuned up. Beyond intent and approving faces, I saw the dark brown hair for a moment, the delicate light-skinned forehead and the firm, red lips. Then I tapped lightly on my stand and we commenced the second movement, which requires no excuses on my part. The players warmed up, the growing yearning in the melody swelled restlessly, spiraled insatiably upward, searched and then became lost in mournful fearfulness. The cello took up the melody with a warm and deep sound, developed it strongly and insistently and introduced it softly into the new lower key, where it faded away despairingly on half-angry-sounding bass notes.

This second movement was my confession, an admission of my longing and dissatisfaction. The third movement was intended to represent satisfaction and fulfillment. But that evening I knew that that was not the case, and I played it carelessly, like something that I knew I was over with. For I thought I now understood exactly how fulfillment should have sounded, how radiance and peace should have emerged through the raging storm of sound, like the light from behind the heavy clouds. All this was not included in my third movement; it was only gentle relief from growing dissonance and an attempt to clarify and strengthen the main theme a little. There was none of the harmony or radiance in it that was now revealed and experienced within me, and I was surprised that no one seemed to notice it.

My trio was finished. I bowed to the other two players and put my violin away. The lights were switched on again and the guests began to stir. Many of them came up to me with the usual polite remarks, praise and criticisms to demonstrate that they were expert judges. No one mentioned the chief fault in the work.

The guests spread out into different rooms. Tea, cakes and wine were served, and the men smoked. One hour passed and then another. At last, what I hardly dared any longer to hope for took place. Gertrude stood before me and held out her hand.

"Did you like it?" I asked.

"Yes, it was beautiful," she said. But I saw that she meant more than that, so I said: "You mean the second movement. The others aren't much."

She looked at me again curiously, with as much sagacity as though she were already a mature woman, and said very delicately: "You know it yourself. The first movement is good music; the second movement is broad and sweeping and demands too much from the third. One could also see as you were playing when your heart was in it and when it was not."

It pleased me to hear that her lovely, bright eyes had observed me without my knowing it. I already thought on that first evening of our meeting how glorious it would be to spend one's whole life regarded by those beautiful, candid eyes, and how it would then be impossible ever to think or do ill. And from that evening I knew that my desire for unity and sweet harmony could be satisfied, and that there was someone on earth whose glance and voice made an instant response to every throb of my pulse and every breath in my body.

She also felt an immediate sympathetic response toward me and right from the beginning was able to be frank and natural with me, without fear of misunderstanding or a breach of confidence. She immediately made friends with me with the speed and ease that is only possible with people who are young and almost unspoiled. Up to that time I had occasionally been attracted to girls, but always — and particularly since my accident — with a shy, wistful and unsure feeling. Now instead of being just infatuated, I was really in love, and it seemed that a thin, gray veil had fallen from my eyes and that the world lay before me in its original divine light as it does to children, and as it appears to us in our dreams of Paradise.

At that time, Gertrude was hardly more than twenty years old, as slender and healthy as a strong young tree. She had passed untouched through the usual turbulence of adolescence, following the dictates of her own noble nature like a clearly developing melody. I felt happy to know a person like her in this imperfect world and I could not think of trying to capture her and keep her for myself. I was glad to be permitted to share her happy youth a little and to know from the beginning that I would be included among her close friends.

During the night after that musical evening I did not fall asleep for a long time. I was not tormented by any fever or feeling of restlessness, but I lay awake and did not wish to sleep because I knew that my springtime had arrived and that after long, wistful, futile wanderings and wintry seasons, my heart was now at rest. My room was filled with the pale glimmer of night. I could see all the goals of life and art lying before me like windswept peaks. I could feel what I had often lost so completely — the harmony and inward rhythm of my life — could feel it in every fiber of my being and trace it back within me to the legendary years of my childhood. And when I wanted to express this dreamlike beauty and sublimity of feeling briefly and call it by a name, then I had to give it the name of Gertrude. That is how I fell asleep when it was already approaching morning, and the next day I awakened refreshed after a long, deep sleep.

I then reflected on my recent feelings of despair and pride, and I realized what had been lacking. Today nothing tormented me or annoyed me. I again heard the ethereal harmony and experienced my youthful dream of the harmony of the spheres. I again walked and thought and breathed to an inward melody; life again had meaning and I looked forward to a better future. No one noticed the change in me; there was no one close enough.

Only Teiser, with his childlike simplicity, gave me a friendly tap on the shoulder during rehearsal at the theater and said: "You slept well last night, didn't you?"

I thought of something to please him and during the next interval I said: "Teiser, where are you going this summer?"

Thereupon he laughed bashfully and flushed as red as an engaged girl who is asked about her wedding day and said:

"Dear me, that's a long way off yet, but look, I have the tickets already." He took them out of his waistcoat pocket. "This time I start from Bodensee; then the Rhine Valley, Fürstentum Liechtenstein, Chur, Albula, Upper Engadine, Maloja, Bergell and Lake Como. I don't know about the return journey yet."

He picked up his violin and looked at me with pride and delight shining out of his blue-gray, childlike eyes, which seemed never to have seen any of the filth and sorrow in the world. I felt a sense of kinship with him and the way he looked forward to his long walking holiday, to freedom and carefree unity with sun, air and earth. In the same way I felt renewed pleasure at the thought of all the paths in my life which lay before me as if illumined by a brilliant new sun, and which I thought I could travel along steadily with bright eyes and a pure heart.

Now, when I look back, it all seems very remote, but I am still conscious of some of the former light, even if it is not so dazzling. Even now, as in the past, it is a comfort to me in times of depression and disperses the dust from my soul when I pronounce the name Gertrude and think of how she came up to me in the music room of her father's house, as lightly as a bird and as naturally as a friend.

That day I visited Muoth, whom I had been avoiding as much as possible since Lottie's painful confession. He had noticed it and was, I knew, too proud and too indifferent to do anything about it, so we had not been alone together for months. Now that I had renewed faith in life and was full of good intentions, it seemed very important to me to approach my neglected friend again. A new song that I had composed gave me an excuse for doing so. I decided to dedicate it to him. It was similar to the Avalanche Song, which he liked, and the words were as follows:

*The hour was late, I blew out my
  candle;
By the open window I greeted the
  night.*

*It embraced me gently, called me
    brother
And promised me friendship in my sad
    plight.*

*We were sick with the same yearning,
Our dreams were gloomy and long,
We whispered about the days of old
When we were young and hope was
    strong.*

I made a copy of it and wrote above it: "Dedicated to my friend, Heinrich Muoth."

Then I went to see him at a time when I knew he would be at home. I heard him singing as he walked up and down rehearsing in his stately rooms. He received me coolly.

"Good heavens, it's Mr. Kuhn! I thought you would not come any more."

"Well," I said, "here I am. How are you?"

"The same as ever. Good of you to come and see me again."

"Yes, I haven't been very loyal recently . . ."

"It has been very evident and I know why."

"I don't think so."

"Yes, I do. Lottie once went to see you, didn't she?"

"Yes, but I don't want to talk about it."

"It isn't at all necessary. Anyway, here you are again."

"I have brought something with me." I gave him the music.

"Oh, a new song! That is good. I was afraid you might devote yourself solely to dreary string music. There's a dedication on it already. What, to me! Do you mean it?"

I was surprised that it seemed to give him so much pleasure. I had somehow expected a joke about the dedication.

"Of course I am pleased," he said sincerely. "I am always glad when worthwhile people think of me, and particularly you. I had really struck you off my list."

"Have you a list?"

"Oh yes, when one has or has had as many friends as I . . . . I could make quite a catalogue. I have always thought most of the highly moral ones and those are always the ones who discard me. One can find friends among rascals any day, but it is difficult to do so among idealists and ordinary people if one has a reputation. You are almost the only one at the moment. And the way things are going — People like best what is hard for them to obtain, don't you agree? I have always wanted friends but it has always been women who have been attracted to me."

"That is partly your own fault, Mr. Muoth."

"Why?"

"You like to treat all people as you do women. It does not work with friends and that is why they leave you. You are an egoist."

"Thank goodness I am. What is more, you are too. When that dreadful Lottie poured out her tale of woe to you, you didn't help her in any way. You also didn't make the incident an excuse for converting me, for which I am grateful. The affair gave you a feeling of aversion and you kept away from me."

"Well, here I am again. You are right, I should have tried to help Lottie, but I don't understand these things. She herself laughed at me and told me I didn't understand anything about love."

"Well, you keep to friendship. It is also a good sphere. Now we'll study the song; sit down and play the accompaniment. Do you remember how it was with your first one? It looks as if you are gradually becoming famous."

"Things are improving, but I will never catch up with you."

"Nonsense, you are a composer, a creator, a little god! What is fame to you? People like me have to be pushy to get anywhere. Singers and tightrope walkers have to do the same as women, take their goods to the market while they are still in good condition. Fame up to the hilt, and money, wine and champagne! Photographs in the newspapers, and bouquets! I tell you, if I became unpopular today, or perhaps had a little inflammation of the lungs, I would be finished tomorrow, and fame and bouquets and all the rest would come to an abrupt end."

"Oh, don't worry about that until it happens."

"Do you know, I'm very curious about growing old. Youth is a real swindle — a swindle of the press and textbooks. 'The most wonderful time of one's life!' Old people always seem much more contented to me. Youth is the most difficult time of life. For example, suicide rarely occurs among old people."

I began to play the piano and he turned his attention to the song. He quickly learned the melody and gave me an appreciative nudge with his elbow at a place where it returned significantly from a minor to a major key.

When I arrived home in the evening, I found, as I had feared, an envelope from Mr. Imthor containing a short, friendly note and a more than substantial fee. I sent the money back and enclosed a note saying I was quite comfortably off and preferred to be allowed to visit his house as a friend. When I saw him again, he invited me to come and visit him again soon and said: "I thought you would feel like that about it. Gertrude said I should not send you anything, but I thought I would just the same."

From that time I was a frequent guest at Imthor's house. I played the first-violin part at many concerts there. I brought new music with me, my own and other people's, and most of my shorter works were first performed there.

One afternoon in spring I found Gertrude at home alone. It was raining, and as I had slipped on the front step on leaving, she would not let me go immediately. We discussed music, and then it happened almost unintentionally that I began to talk to her confidentially, in particular about the grim period I had gone through, during which I had composed my first songs. Then I felt embarrassed and did not know whether I had been wise in making this confession to the girl. Gertrude said to me almost timorously: "I have something to confess which I hope you will not take amiss. I have made copies of two of your songs and learned them."

"Do you sing?" I exclaimed with

surprise. At the same time I remembered with amusement the incident of my first youthful love, and how it ended when I heard the girl sing so badly.

Gertrude smiled and nodded: "Oh yes, I sing, although only for one or two friends and for my own pleasure. I will sing your songs if you will accompany me on the piano."

We went to the piano and she handed me the music, which she had copied in her neat, feminine hand. I began the accompaniment softly, so that I could listen to her. She sang one song, then another, and I listened and heard my music changed and transformed. She sang in a high, pure voice, and it was the sweetest thing I had ever heard in my life. Her voice went through me like the south wind across a snow-covered valley, and every note made my heart feel lighter. Although I felt happy and almost as if floating on air, I had to control myself, for there were tears in my eyes which nearly obliterated the music.

I thought I had known what love was, and had felt wise in my knowledge. I had looked at the world with new eyes and felt a closer kinship toward all people. Now it was different; now there was no longer light, solace and pleasure, but storm and flame. My heart now exulted, beat more quickly and did not want to know anything more about life; it just wanted to consume itself in its own flame. If anyone had now asked me what love was, I should have been able to describe it, and it would have sounded ardent and tumultuous.

In the meantime, I could hear Gertrude's voice rising. It seemed to call me and wish to give me pleasure, and yet it soared to remote heights, inaccessible and almost alien to me. I now understood how things were with me. She could sing, be friendly, and think well of me, but all this was not what I wanted. If she could not be mine alone, completely and forever, then I lived in vain, and everything that was good and fine and genuine in me had no meaning.

I then felt her hand on my shoulder. I was startled, turned round and looked at her. Her bright eyes were serious, and only after a short time, as I continued to gaze at her, did she smile sweetly and blush.

I could only say thank you. She did not know what was the matter with me. She realized only that I was deeply affected and tactfully picked up the threads of our previous pleasant, easy-flowing conversation. I left shortly afterward.

I went home and did not know whether it was still raining. I walked through the streets leaning on my stick, and yet I did not really walk and the streets seemed unreal. I traveled on stormy clouds across a changing, darkened sky. I talked to the storm and was myself the storm, and coming from above me in the remote distance I thought I heard something. It was a woman's high, sweet voice and it seemed quite immune from human thoughts and emotions, and yet at the same time it seemed to have all the wild sweetness of passion in its essence.

That evening I sat in my room without a light. As I could not endure it any longer — it was already late — I went to Muoth's house. When I found his windows in darkness, I turned back. I walked about for a long time in the night, and finally found myself, wearily coming back to earth, outside the Imthors' garden. The old trees rustled solemnly around the concealed house from which no sound or light penetrated, and pale stars emerged here and there among the clouds.

I waited several days before I ventured to go and see Gertrude again. During this time I received a letter from the poet whose poems I had set to music. We had communicated with each other for two years and I occasionally received interesting letters from him. I sent him my music and he sent me his poems. He now wrote:

Dear Sir,

I have not written to you for some time. I have been very busy. Ever since I have become familiar with your music, I have had a text in mind for you, but it would not form itself. Now I have it and it is almost ready. It is a libretto for an opera, and you must compose the music for it. I gather you are not a particularly happy person; that is revealed in your music. I will not speak about myself, but this text is just for you. As there is nothing else to make us rejoice, let us present something good to the public, something which will make it clear, even to those who are thick-skinned, that life is not lived on the surface alone. As we do not really know ourselves where to begin, it worries us to be aware of the wasted powers of others.

HANS H.

It fell like a spark in gunpowder. I wrote for the libretto and was so impatient that I tore up my letter and sent a telegram. The manuscript arrived a week later. It was a passionate love story written in verse. There were still gaps in it, but it was sufficient for me for the time being. I read it and went about with the verses going through my head. I sang them and tried music to them on the violin day and night. Shortly afterwards I went to see Gertrude.

"You must help me," I cried. "I am composing an opera. Here are three arias suitable for your voice. Will you have a look at them and sing them for me sometime?"

She seemed very pleased, asked me to tell her about it, glanced at the music and promised to learn the arias soon. Then followed a wonderful, fruitful period; intoxicated with love and music, I was incapable of thinking of anything else, and Gertrude was the only one who knew my secret about the opera. I took the music to her and she learned it and sang it. I consulted her about it, played everything to her, and she shared my enthusiasm, studied and sang, advised and helped me, and enjoyed the secret and the growing work that belonged to us both. There was no point or suggestion which she did not immediately understand and assimilate. Later she began to help me with copying and rewriting music in her neat hand. I had taken sick leave from the theater.

No feeling of embarrassment arose between Gertrude and me. We were swept along by the same current and worked for the same end. It was for her, as it was for me, the blossoming of maturing powers, a period of happiness and magic in which my passions worked unseen. She did not distinguish between me and my work. She found pleasure in us both and belonged to us both. For me too love and work, music and life, were no longer separable. Sometimes I looked at the lovely girl with astonishment and admiration, and she would return my glance, and whenever I came or departed, she pressed my hand more warmly and firmly than I ventured to press hers. And whenever I walked through the garden and entered the old house during those mild spring days, I did not know whether it was my work or my love which impelled and exalted me.

Times like those do not last long. This one was approaching the end, and the flame within me steadily flared up into many confused desires. I sat at her piano and she sang the last act of my opera, the soprano part of which was completed. She sang beautifully, and while her voice soared, I reflected upon the glorious days that I felt were already changing, and knew that inevitably different and more clouded days were on the way. Then she smiled at me and leaned toward me in connection with the music. She noticed the sad expression on my face and looked at me questioningly. I did not say anything. I stood up, held her face gently in both hands, kissed her on the forehead and on the mouth and then sat down again. She permitted all this quietly and almost solemnly, without surprise or annoyance, and when she saw tears in my eyes, she gently stroked my hair, forehead and shoulder with her soft, smooth hand.

Then I began to play the piano and she sang again, and the kiss and that wonderful hour remained unmentioned, though unforgotten, as our final secret.

The other secret could not remain between us much longer; the opera now required other people and assistants. The first one must be Muoth, as I had thought of him for the principal character, whose impetuosity and violent emotions could well be interpreted with Muoth's voice and personality. I delayed doing anything for a short time. My work was still a bond between Gertrude and me. It belonged to us both and brought us both pleasures and cares. It was like a garden unknown to anyone else, or a ship on which we two alone crossed a great ocean.

She asked me about it herself when she felt and saw that she could not help me further.

"Who will sing the principal part?" she asked.

"Heinrich Muoth."

She seemed surprised. "Oh," she said, "are you serious? I don't like him."

"He is a friend of mine, Miss Gertrude, and he would be suitable for the part."

"Oh!"

A stranger had already come between us.

Chapter Five

Meanwhile, I had not thought about Muoth's holidays and love of traveling. He was very pleased about my plans for an opera and promised to help me as much as possible, but he was occupied with traveling plans and could only promise to go through his part for the autumn. I copied it out for him as far as it was ready. He took it with him and as usual I did not hear anything from him all those months.

So we had a respite. A very pleasant relationship now existed between Gertrude and me. I believe that, since that time at the piano, she knew quite well what was going on inside me, but she never said a word and was not different with me in any way. She did not like only my music, she liked me too, and felt as I did, that there was a natural bond between us and a feeling of mutual understanding and affection. Her behavior toward me was therefore kind and friendly, but without passion. At times that was sufficient for me and I spent quiet, contented days in her company, but passion always soon arose as the additional factor between us, and her friendliness then seemed only like charity to me and it tormented me to see that the waves of love and desire that overpowered me were alien and disagreeable to her. Often I deceived myself and tried to persuade myself that she had a placid, unemotional temperament. Yet in my heart I felt it was not true, and I knew Gertrude well enough to know that love would also bring her hazards and a tumult of emotions. I often thought about it later and felt that if I had taken her by storm, fought for her, and drawn her to me with all my strength, she would have followed me and gone with me for good. But I mistrusted her pleasant manner toward me, and when she was gentle and showed affection for me, I attributed it to the usual undesired sympathy. I could not rid myself of the thought that if she had liked a healthy, attractive man as much as she liked me, she could not have maintained the relationship on this quiet, friendly basis for so long. It was then not rare for me to spend hours feeling that I would have exchanged my music and all that was of value to me for a straight leg and a gay disposition.

About that time Teiser drew closer to me again. He was indispensable for my work, and so he was the next one to learn my secret and become familiar with the libretto and my plans for an opera. He was very discreet about it all and took the work home to study. When he came again, his childlike face with its fair beard beamed with pleasure and excitement about the music.

"That opera of yours is going to be something!" he exclaimed with excitement. "I can already feel the overture in my fingertips. Now, let's go and have a drink, you rascal. If it were not too presumptuous, I would suggest that we drink a pledge of brotherhood — but I don't want to force it on you."

I willingly accepted the invitation and we had a pleasant evening together. For the first time Teiser took me home with him. His sister, who had been left alone at her mother's death, had recently come to live with him. Teiser could not speak highly enough of the comfort of his changed household after his long bachelor years. His sister was a quiet, pleasant girl, with the same bright, childlike eyes as her brother. She was called Brigitte. She brought us cakes and clear Austrian wine, also a box of long Virginia cigars. We drank the first glass of wine to her health and the second to our good friendship, and while we ate cakes, drank wine and smoked, Teiser moved delightedly about the room. First he sat down by the piano, then on the settee with a guitar, then at the end of the table with his violin, and played anything pleasant that was going through his head. He sang too and his bright eyes sparkled and it was all a tribute to me and to the opera. It seemed that his sister had the same blood in her veins and swore no less by Mozart than he did. Arias from *The Magic Flute* and excerpts from *Don Giovanni,* interrupted now and then by conversation and the clinking of glasses, echoed through the little house, beautifully accompanied by her brother on the violin, piano or guitar, or even just by whistling.

I was still engaged as a violinist in the orchestra for the short summer season, but had asked for my release in the autumn, as I wished to devote all my time and energy to my work. The conductor, who was annoyed because I was leaving, was very rude to me toward the end, but Teiser helped me greatly to defend myself and to rise above it.

With the help of this loyal friend, I worked at the orchestration of my opera. While respecting my ideas, he rigorously put his finger on all the technical errors. Often he became quite annoyed and rebuked me like an outspoken conductor, until the doubtful part which

I had liked and wished to retain was crossed out and altered. He was always ready with examples whenever I was in doubt. When I presented something unsatisfactorily or was not venturesome enough, he came running to me with scores and showed me how Mozart or Lortzing would have handled it, and proved to me that my hesitation was cowardice, or my obstinacy audacious stupidity. We bellowed at each other, disputed and grew excited, and if it occurred in Teiser's house, Brigitte listened to us attentively, came to and fro with wine and cigars, and smoothed out many crumpled sheets of music carefully and sympathetically. Her admiration for me was equal to her affection for her brother; to her I was a maestro. Every Sunday I was invited to lunch at the Teisers'. After the meal, even if there was only a tiny blue patch in the sky, we took the tram to the outskirts of town. Then we walked over the hills and through the woods, talked and sang, and the Teisers frequently yodeled in their native fashion.

We once stopped for a light meal in the garden of a village inn, where the merry music of a country dance drifted across to us through the wide-open windows. When we had eaten and sat resting over our cider, Brigitte slipped across to the house and went inside. We watched her do this and soon after we saw her dance past the window, as fresh and sparkling as a summer morning. When she returned, Teiser shook his finger at her and said she should have asked him to go along too. She then blushed and became embarrassed, shook her head protestingly and looked at me.

"What's the matter?" asked her brother.

"Nothing," she said, but by chance I saw how she made him realize the significance of her glance, and Teiser said: "Oh, of course!"

I did not say anything, but it seemed strange to me to see her embarrassed because she had danced while I was there. For the first time it occurred to me that their walks also would have been quicker and longer if I had not been there to restrict them, and after that I only joined them occasionally on their Sunday excursions.

When he had gone through the soprano part as far as possible, Gertrude noticed that I was reluctant to give up my frequent visits to her and our pleasant times together at the piano, and that yet I was too shy to make excuses for their continuation. Then she surprised me with the suggestion that I should visit her regularly to accompany her singing, and I now went to her house two or three times a week in the afternoons. Her father was pleased at her friendship with me. Gertrude had lost her mother when she was still young; she was mistress of the house and her father let her have her own way in everything.

The garden was in its full splendor. It abounded with flowers, and birds sang around the quiet house. When I entered the garden from the road and went past the old, darkened statues in the drive toward the house, which was surrounded by greenery, it was for me each time like entering a sanctuary, where the voices and things of the world could only penetrate to a slight degree. The bees hummed among the flowering bushes in front of the windows, sunshine and the soft shadows of the foliage dappled the room, and I sat at the piano and heard Gertrude sing. I listened to her voice, which rose easily and without effort, and when after a song we looked at each other and smiled, it was in a united and confiding way as if between brother and sister. I often felt at these times that I had only to stretch out my hands to grasp my happiness and have it for good, and yet I did not do so, because I wanted to wait until she also showed some sign of desire and longing. But Gertrude seemed to be contented and not to wish for anything else. Indeed, it often seemed to me that she did not wish to shatter this peaceful relationship and disturb the springtime of our friendship.

If I was disappointed about this, it was a consolation to me to know how deeply she cared for my music, how well she understood and was proud of it.

This state of affairs lasted until June. Then Gertrude and her father went off into the mountains. I remained behind, and whenever I went past her house, I saw it standing empty behind the plane trees, with the gate locked. The pain returned, grew and followed me into the night.

In the evenings I went to the Teisers, almost always with music in my case, and shared their quiet, contented way of life. I drank their Austrian wine and played Mozart with them. Afterwards I walked back in the mild night, saw couples walking about in the parks, went home wearily to bed but could not sleep. It was now inconceivable to me that I could have behaved in such a brotherly fashion toward Gertrude and that I had never broken down the barrier, drawn her to me, taken her by storm and won her. I could imagine her in her light-blue or gray dress, merry or serious; I could hear her voice, and could not conceive ever having heard it without being filled with passion and a desire to make love to her.

Restless and agitated, I rose, switched on the light and threw myself into my work. I made human voices and instruments woo, plead and threaten. I repeated the song of yearning in new, feverish melodies. Often this comfort also was lacking to me, and afterwards, when I lay in bed, ardent and restless, in a state of wretched sleeplessness, I uttered her name, "Gertrude, Gertrude," wildly and senselessly, thrust comfort and hope aside and surrendered myself despairingly to the dreadful prostration of desire. I cried out to God and asked him why he had made me this way, why he had made me a cripple, and why instead of the happiness that was the lot of the poorest of mortals, he had given me nothing but the terrible solace of living in a whirl of sounds where, in the face of my desires, I continually depicted the unattainable in strange fantasies.

During the day I was more successful in controlling my emotions. I clenched my teeth, sat at my work from the early hours of the morning, calmed myself by taking long walks and refreshed myself with cold shower baths. In the evenings I fled from the shadows of the approaching night to the cheerful company of the Teisers, with whom I obtained a few hours of rest and sometimes pleasure. Teiser noticed that I was ill and suffering and put it down to all the work. He advised me to rest awhile, although he himself was full of enthusiasm and inwardly was as excited and impatient as I was to see the opera growing. Sometimes I also called for him and spent an evening with him alone in the cool garden of some inn, but even then I was disturbed by the sight of young lovers, Chinese lanterns and fireworks, and the fragrance of desire in the air which always hovers over towns on summer evenings.

It was worst of all when Teiser also went away to spend his holidays with Brigitte walking among the mountains. He invited me to come along too, and he meant it seriously, although my inability to move about easily would have spoiled his pleasure; but I could not accept his invitation.

For two weeks I remained in town alone, miserable and unable to sleep, and I did not make any further progress with my work.

Then Gertrude sent me a small box full of Alpine roses from a village in Wallis. When I saw her handwriting and unpacked the brownish, fading flowers, it was like a glance from her dear eyes and I felt ashamed of my agitation and lack of confidence. I decided it was better for her to know how I felt, and the next morning I wrote her a short letter. I told her half jokingly that I could not sleep and that it was through longing for her, and that I could no longer just be friendly with her, as I was in love with her. While writing, I was again overcome by my emotions, and the letter, which had started mildly and almost jestingly, ended impetuously and ardently.

Almost every day the post brought me greetings and picture postcards from the Teisers, who naturally could not know that their cards and letters brought me disappointment each time, for I was waiting to hear from someone else.

It came at last, a gray envelope with Gertrude's clear, flowing handwriting on it, and inside was a letter.

My dear friend,
   Your letter has embarrassed me. I realize that you are suffering, otherwise I would scold you for attacking me in this way. You know I am very fond of you, but I am quite contented with my present state and have as yet no desire to change it. If I thought there was any danger of losing you, I would do everything possible to prevent it. But I can give no reply to your ardent letter. Be patient, let things remain between us as they were until we can see each other again and talk things over. Everything will then be easier.
                    Yours affectionately,
                              GERTRUDE

It had altered the position very little and yet the letter made me happier. After all, it was a greeting from her; she had permitted me to make a declaration of love and had not snubbed me. The letter also seemed to bring some of her personality with it, some of her almost cool sweetness, and instead of the image of her which my longing had created, she was again in my thoughts as her real self. Her words seemed to ask for confidence from me. I felt as if she were near me and immediately I was aware of both shame and pride. It helped me to conquer my tormenting longings and to suppress my burning desires. Uncomforted, but strengthened and more in command of myself, I held my head high. I obtained accommodation in a village inn, two hours' traveling distance from the town, and took my work with me. I sat meditating a great deal in a cool, already faded lilac bower, and thought quite often about my life. How strange and lonely was my path and how uncertain my destination! Nowhere did I have any roots and a place I could really call home. I kept up only a superficial relationship with my parents by means of polite letters. I had even given up my occupation in order to indulge in creating hazardous fantasies, which did not completely satisfy me. My friends did not really understand me. Gertrude was the only person with whom I could have had complete understanding and a perfect relationship. And was I not just chasing shadows and building castles in the air with the work for which I lived and which should have given meaning to my life? Could it really have a meaning and justify and fill a person's life, this building up of sound patterns and the exciting play with images, which at the best would help other people to pass a pleasant hour?

Nevertheless, I worked fairly hard again during that summer. I completed the opera inwardly, even though there was still much detail lacking and only a small part of the work had been written out. Sometimes it gave me great pleasure and I thought with pride how my work would have power over people, how singers and musicians, conductors and choruses would have to act in accordance with my wishes, and how the opera would have an effect on thousands of people. At other times it seemed even ominous and nightmarish to me that all this power and emotion should arise from the restless dreams and imagination of a poor lonely man whom everyone pitied. At other times I lost courage and felt that my opera would never be performed, that it was all unreal and exaggerated. But this feeling was rare; in my heart I was convinced of the quality and strength of my work. It was sincere and ardent; it had been experienced and had blood in its veins. If I do not want to hear it any more nowadays and write quite a different kind of music, nevertheless all my youth is in that opera. Whenever I hear melodies from it, it is as if a mild spring storm drifts across to me from the abandoned valleys of youth and passion. And when I think that all its strength and power over people was born of weakness, privation and longing, I no longer know whether my whole life at that time, and also at present, can be called happy or sad.

Summer was approaching its end. One

dark night, during a heavy, tempestuous downpour of rain, I finished writing the overture. The following morning, the rain was slight and cool, the sky an even gray, and the garden had become autumnal. I packed my possessions and went back to town.

Among my acquaintances, Teiser and his sister were the only ones who had already returned. They both looked very well and tanned by the mountain sun. They had had a surprising number of experiences on their tour and yet they were very interested and excited to know how my opera was progressing. We went through the overture and it was quite a moment for me when Teiser put his hand on my shoulder and said: "Look, Brigitte, here is a great musician!"

Despite all my yearning and ardor, I awaited Gertrude's return with great eagerness, as I had a large amount of work to show her. I knew that she would take a keen interest in it, and understand and enjoy it all as if it were her own. Above all, I was anxious to see Heinrich Muoth, whose help was essential to me and from whom I had not heard for months.

Finally Muoth arrived before Gertrude did and walked into my room one morning. He looked at me searchingly.

"You look terrible," he said, shaking his head. "Well, when one composes music like that!"

"Have you looked at your part?"

"Looked at it? I know it by heart and will sing it as soon as you wish. It's extraordinary music!"

"Do you really think so?"

"I do. You have been doing your finest work. Just wait! Your moderate fame will be a thing of the past when your opera is performed. Well, that's your affair. When do you want me to sing? There are one or two points that I want to mention. How far are you with the whole opera?"

I showed him my work and he then took me to his rooms. There, for the first time, I heard him sing the part for which I had always had him in mind during the play of my own emotions, and I felt the power of my music and his singing. Only now could I visualize the whole opera on the stage, only now could my own flame reach me and let me feel its warmth. It was as if the opera did not belong to me, as if it had never been my work but had its own life and the effect of an external power over me. For the first time I felt this sense of detachment of a work from its creator, in which I had not previously really believed. My work began to stand up, move and show signs of life. A moment ago I had still held it in my hand; now it was no longer mine; it was like a child that had grown taller than its father; it lived and acted of its own accord and looked at me independently through its own eyes; yet it bore my name and my imprint. I experienced the same conflicting, sometimes frightening, sensation when my works were performed later on.

Muoth had learned the part very well, and I was easily able to give my agreement to the slight alterations he desired. He then inquired about the soprano part, which he knew only partly, and wished to know whether a singer had yet tried it. For the first time I had to tell him about Gertrude, and I managed to do so quietly and casually. He knew the name quite well, although he had never been to Imthor's house. He was surprised to hear that Gertrude had studied the part and could sing it.

"She must have a good voice," he said approvingly, "high and sweet. Will you take me there sometime?"

"I intended in any case to ask them if you could come. I should like to hear you sing with Miss Imthor once or twice; some corrections will be necessary. As soon as the Imthors are back in town, I will ask them."

"You're a lucky fellow really, Kuhn. And Teiser will be able to help you with the orchestration. The opera will be a success, you'll see."

I did not say anything. I had as yet no thoughts about the future and the fate of my opera; first of all, it must be finished. But since I had heard him sing it, I also believed in the power of my work.

When I told Teiser about it, he said grimly: "I can believe you. Muoth has tremendous energy. If only he weren't such a faker. He never really cares about the music, only about himself. He is a complete egoist."

On the day that I went to see Gertrude, who had at last returned, my heart beat more quickly as I walked through the garden of the Imthors' house in its autumnal garb, with the leaves already beginning to fall. But she came toward me smiling, looking a little sunburned and more beautiful and graceful than ever. She held out her hand to me, and her dear voice, her bright eyes and her whole charming, natural manner immediately bewitched me anew. I gladly put my sorrows and desires aside and was happy to be in her soothing presence again. She did not press me, and as I could not bring myself to mention my letter and the nature of it, she also remained silent about it, and in no way indicated by her behavior that our friendship was in any way spoiled or in danger. She did not try to avoid me; she was often alone with me, as she was confident that I would respect her wishes and not repeat my declaration of love unless she encouraged me. Without wasting any time, we went through my work of the last few months and I told her that Muoth had learned his part and praised it. I asked her permission to bring him there, as it was essential for me to go through both principal parts with them together, and she gave her agreement.

"I am not doing so willingly," she said. "You know that I never sing for strangers, and before Heinrich Muoth it will be doubly painful, and not just because he is a famous singer. There is something about him that frightens me, at least on the stage. Anyway, we'll see how it goes."

I did not venture to defend and praise my friend. I did not want to make her feel more embarrassed and I was convinced that, after the first time, she would willingly sing with him again.

Several days later, Muoth and I went to the Imthors' and were received by our host with great politeness and reserve. He had never shown the slightest objection to my frequent visits and my friendship with Gertrude and would have laughed if anyone had said anything against it. He was less pleased about Muoth coming, but the latter's manner was very polished and correct and both Imthors were agreeably disappointed. The forceful, arrogant singer with a bad reputation could behave irreproachably. Also he was not vain and decided in his opinions, but modest.

"Shall we sing?" asked Gertrude after a while. We stood up and went across to the music room. I sat down at the piano, said a few words about the introduction and scene, gave some directions and then asked Gertrude to begin. She did so, singing softly in a restrained and careful manner. On the other hand, when it was Muoth's turn to sing, he did so aloud without hesitation or selfconsciousness, captivated us both and made us enter the spirit of the music so that Gertrude now also sang without restraint. Muoth, who was used to treating ladies of good family very formally, now paid attention to her, listened to her singing with interest, and expressed his admiration in encouraging but not exaggerated words.

From then on all prejudices vanished; the music drew us together and we were of one mind. And my work that lay there half dead in imperfectly connected parts continued to assume the shape of a whole and living thing. I now knew that the chief part of the work was done, that there was nothing of importance that could spoil it, and it seemed good to me. I did not conceal my pleasure and gratefully thanked both my friends. Muoth and I left the house in a festive mood and he treated me to an unexpected celebration at the inn where he was staying. While we drank champagne, he did something that he was a little afraid to do; he addressed me as an intimate friend and continued to do so. This pleased me and had my approval.

"Here we are enjoying ourselves and celebrating," he said, laughing, "and I think it is a good idea to do it in advance. That is the best time. Afterward things seem different. You are going to be in the limelight, young fellow, and I hope it doesn't spoil you as it does most people."

Gertrude was still ill at ease with Muoth for a long time, and only while singing with him was she natural and unrestrained. He was very polite and considerate, and gradually Gertrude was glad to see him and invited him each time in a friendly fashion to come again, just as she did with me. The occasions on which the three of us were alone together became less frequent. The parts had been learned and discussed and, moreover, the Imthors, now that it was winter, had resumed their conviviality, with regular musical evenings. Muoth often appeared at these gatherings but without ever singing.

At times I thought that Gertrude was beginning to be more reserved with me and that she was to some extent drawing away from me. However, I always reproached myself for these thoughts and was ashamed of my suspicions. Gertrude was very much in demand as the mistress of a house where much entertaining was done, and if often gave me pleasure to see her move about and act as hostess among her guests, looking so young, charming and gracious.

The weeks passed by very quickly for me. I worked at my opera, which I hoped to finish during the winter. I had meetings with Teiser, and spent many evenings with him and his sister. Then there were all sorts of letters and arrangements, as my songs were sung at different places and all the string music I had composed was played in Berlin. There were inquiries and newspaper reviews, and suddenly everyone seemed to know that I was working on an opera, although, apart from Gertrude, the Teisers and Muoth, I had not said a word about it to anyone. It did not really matter and inwardly I was happy about these signs of success. It seemed as if at last, and yet soon enough, a path lay open before me.

I had not been to my parents' house for a whole year and I went there for Christmas. My mother was affectionate, but there was the old reserve between us, which on my side was a fear of being misunderstood, and on her side a lack of faith in my career as a musician and disbelief in the seriousness of my endeavors. She now talked animatedly about what she had heard and read about me, but more to give me pleasure than from conviction, for inwardly she mistrusted these apparent successes as much as she did my art as a whole. It was not that she did not like music — indeed at one time she used to sing a little — but in her opinion a musician was a poor sort of person. She had also heard some of my music and did not understand or care for it.

My father had more faith. As a merchant he thought above all of my material success, and although he had always given me a generous allowance without grumbling and had again continued to support me fully when I left the orchestra, he was glad to see that I was beginning to earn money and that there were prospects of my making a living by my own efforts. Having made money himself, he regarded this as an essential basis for a respectable existence. He was in bed when I arrived. He had had a fall the day before my arrival and had injured his foot.

I found him tending toward slightly philosophical conversations. I came closer to him than ever and took delight in his practical outlook on life. I was able to tell him many of my troubles, which I had never done before because of a sense of bashfulness. Something Muoth had once said occurred to me and I repeated it to my father. Muoth had said, not really in earnest, that he thought youth was the most difficult time of life and he found that most old people were much more serene and contented than young people. My father laughed at that and said thoughtfully: "Naturally we old people say just the opposite, but there is some truth in what your friend said. I think one can draw quite a distinct division between youth and maturity. Youth ends when egotism does; maturity begins when one lives for others. That is what I mean. Young people have many pleasures and many sorrows, because they have only themselves to think of, so every wish and every notion assumes importance; every pleasure is tasted to the full but also every sorrow, and many who find that their wishes cannot be fulfilled, put an end immediately to their lives. That is being young. To most people, however, there comes a time when the situation changes, when they live more for others, not for any virtuous reasons, but quite naturaly. A family is the reason with most people. One thinks less about oneself and one's wishes when one has a family. Others lose their egotism in a responsible position, in politics, in art or in science. Young people want to play; mature people want to work. A man does not marry just to have children, but if he has them they change him, and finally he sees that everything has happened just for them. That links up with the fact that young people like to talk about death but do not really think about it. It is just the other way round with old people. Life seems long to young people and they can therefore concentrate all their wishes and thoughts on themselves. Old people are conscious of an approaching end, and that everything one has and does solely for oneself finally falls short and lacks value. Therefore a man requires a different kind of continuity and faith; he does not work just for the worms. That is why one has a wife and children, business and responsibility, so that one knows for whom one endures the daily toil. In that respect your friend is quite right, a man is happier when he lives for others than when he lives just for himself, but old people should not make it out to be such an act of heroism, because it isn't one really. In any case, the most lively young people become the best old people, not those who pretend to be as wise as grandfathers while they are still at school."

I remained at home for a week and sat a great deal at my father's bedside. He was not a patient invalid; besides, except for the small injury to his foot, he was in excellent health. I told him I was sorry that I had not confided in him more and drawn closer to him before, but he remarked that that could be said for both sides, and our relationship in the future would be better than if we had made premature attempts to understand each other, which rarely succeed. In a discreet and kind way, he asked me whether I'd had any luck with women. I did not want to say anything about Gertrude; what I did tell him was very brief.

"Don't worry," said my father, smiling. "You are the type to make a really good husband; intelligent women will soon notice that. Only be wary of women of small means who may be after your money. And if you do not find the one that you envisage and think you would like, it is still not disastrous. Love between young people and love after many years of marriage is not the same thing. When one is young, one has only oneself to think of and care for, but when there is a household, there are other things to attend to. That is how it was with me, as you well know. I was very much in love with your mother; it was a real love match. But it only lasted a year or two; then our passion died down and was almost spent and we hardly knew where we stood in relation to each other. Then the children came, your two elder sisters, who died when they were young, and we had them to look after. Our demands on each other were consequently less, the coolness between us came to an end, and suddenly love was there again; to be sure, it was not the old love, but something quite new. This has lasted without needing much reviving for more than thirty years. Not all love matches turn out as well. Indeed, very few do."

To me, all these observations served no purpose, but the new cordial relationship with my father encouraged me and made me again enjoy my home, toward which I had felt almost indifferent during the past few years. When I departed, I did not regret the visit and decided to keep in more frequent contact with the old people in the future.

Work and traveling for performances of my string music prevented me from visiting the Imthors for a while. When I went there again, I found that Muoth, who had previously gone there only in my company, was now among the most frequently invited guests. Mr. Imthor still treated him coolly and rather distantly, but Gertrude seemed to have become good friends with him. I was glad about that. I saw no grounds for jealousy and was convinced that two people who were as dissimilar as Muoth and Gertrude would interest and attract each other but could not love and make each other happy. So I was not at all suspicious when he sang with her and their beautiful voices mingled. They looked attractive together; they were both tall and well-formed, he morose and serious, she bright and serene. Eventually, however, it seemed to me that she found some difficulty in maintaining her old innate serenity, and she sometimes seemed tired and distracted. Quite often she looked at me seriously and searchingly, with curiosity and interest, in the way that worried and depressed people look at each other, and when I smiled at her and responded with a friendly look, her features relaxed into a smile so slowly and in such a forced manner that I was disturbbed.

Yet it was quite rare that I noticed this; at other times Gertrude looked as cheerful and radiant as ever, so that I attributed these observations to imagination or a passing indisposition. Only once was I really shocked. While one of her guests was playing some Beethoven, she leaned back in the semi-darkness, probably thinking that she was quite unobserved. Earlier, while receiving her guests in the full light, she had appeared bright and cheerful, but now, withdrawn into herself and clearly unmoved by the music, her face relaxed and assumed an expression of weariness, anxiety and fear, like that of an exasperated child. It lasted several minutes and I was stunned when I saw it. Something was troubling her. That alone was bad, but it worried me that she should pretend to be cheerful and conceal everything from me. As soon as the music was finished, I went up to her, sat down beside her and began a casual conversation. I said that she had had a busy winter and that I had also had a trying time, but my remarks were made in light and half-jesting tones. Finally, I mentioned that period in the spring when we had discussed the beginnings of my opera and had played and sung them together.

She then said: "Yes, those were happy times." She said no more than that, but it was a confession, for she said it with great earnestness. I read in it hope for myself and in my heart I was thankful.

I longed to repeat the question I had asked her during the summer. I believed with all due modesty that I could venture to interpret the change in her manner, the embarrassment and uncertain fears which she revealed at times, as signs favorable to me. I found it touching to see how her girlish pride seemed wounded and hard to disguise. I did not dare say anything; her uncertainty hurt me and I felt I ought to keep my unspoken promise. I have never known how to behave with women. I made the same mistake as Heinrich Muoth, the other way round: I treated women as if they were friends.

As I eventually could not consider my observations to be illusions, and yet only half understood Gertrude's changed manner, I became rather reserved, visited her less frequently and avoided intimate conversations with her. I wanted to show her consideration and not make her more shy and fearful, as she seemed to be suffering and in a state of conflict. I think she noticed the change in my behavior and did not seem displeased that I should keep my distance. I hoped that we should again have a quiet, peaceful time after the winter and the repeated entertaining, and I wanted to wait until then. But I was often very sorry for her, and gradually I also felt disturbed and thought there must be something serious pending.

I was restless under the tension of the circumstances. February arrived and I began to long for spring. Muoth had not been to see me very much. He had, indeed, had a strenuous winter at the Opera House and had recently received two important offers from well-known theaters, about which he had to make a decision. He did not seem to have another lady friend; at least, since the break with Lottie I had not seen any other woman at his house. We had recently celebrated his birthday. Since then I had not seen him.

I now felt an urge to go and see him. I was beginning to feel the strain of my changed relationship with Gertrude, overwork and the long winter, and I dropped by to have a chat with him. He gave me a glass of sherry and talked to me about the theater. He seemed tired and distracted and unusually gentle. I listened to him, looked around the room and was just going to ask him whether he had been to the Imthors again, when I accidentally saw an envelope with Gertrude's handwriting on it lying on the table. Before I could really take it in, a feeling of horror and bitterness welled up in me. It could have been an invitation, a simple formality, yet I could not believe this, however much I tried.

I was able to compose myself and left

soon afterward. Almost unwillingly, I realized that I knew everything. It could have been an invitation, a triviality, something quite casual — yet I knew that it was not. Suddenly I clearly understood everything that had happened recently. I made up my mind to wait and make sure, but all my thoughts in this connection were nothing but pretexts and excuses. The arrow had pierced deeply and festered in my blood. When I reached home and sat in my room, my confusion was slowly replaced by a feeling of almost terrible calmness, which finally prevailed, and I knew that my life had been shattered and faith and hope had been destroyed.

For several days I could neither shed a tear nor feel any grief. Without thinking it over, I had decided not to go on living. In any case, the will to live had abandoned me and seemed to have disappeared. I thought about dying as a piece of work that had to be done unhesitatingly, without thinking whether it was pleasant or not.

Among the things I wanted to do

beforehand was first of all to go and visit Gertrude — to a certain extent for the sake of order — to receive the necessary confirmation of my suspicions. I could have had this from Muoth, but although he appeared to be less to blame than Gertrude, I could not bring myself to go to him. I went to see Gertrude but did not find her in. I went again the following day and talked to her and her father for a few minutes, until the latter left us alone together, thinking we wished to practice some music.

She then stood alone before me and I looked at her curiously. She seemed a little changed but no less beautiful than ever.

"Forgive me, Gertrude," I said firmly, "if I trouble you once more. I wrote you a letter during the summer — could I now have an answer to it? I have to go on a journey, perhaps for a long time. Otherwise I should have waited until you yourself . . ."

As she went pale and looked at me in surprise, I helped her and spoke again: "Your answer is no, isn't it? I thought so.

I only wanted to be certain."

She nodded sadly.

"Is it Heinrich?" I asked.

She nodded again, and suddenly she seemed frightened and seized my hand. "Please forgive me and don't do anything to him."

"I don't intend to, you can rest assured," I said and had to smile, for I thought of Marian and Lottie, who had also been so attached to him and whom he had beaten. Perhaps he would also beat Gertrude and destroy her lofty pride and trusting nature.

"Gertrude," I began again, "think it over! Not for my sake. I know now how things stand with me. But Muoth will not make you happy. Goodbye, Gertrude."

My feeling of numbness and unnatural calm persisted. Only now, when Gertrude talked to me this way, in the same tone that I recalled Lottie using, and looked at me so anxiously and said: "Don't go like that. I don't deserve this from you," did I feel as if my heart were breaking, and I had difficulty controlling myself.

I held out my hand to her and said: "I don't want to hurt either you or Heinrich. But wait a little. Don't let him exercise his power over you. He destroys everyone he is fond of."

She shook her head and released my hand. "Goodbye!" she said quietly. "It is not my fault. Think kindly of me and also of Heinrich."

It was over. I went home and proceeded with my plan as if it were a piece of work to be done. It was true that while I did this my heart was heavy and filled to the brim with sorrow, but I was aware of it in a remote way and had no spare thoughts for it. It was all the same to me whether the days and hours that were left went well or not. I put in order the pile of sheets on which my half-finished opera was written, and wrote a letter to Teiser to go with it, so that my work should, if possible, be preserved. Then I seriously considered the manner in which I should die. I wished to spare my parents, but could think of no manner of dying that would make this possible. ·In the long run, it did not matter so much. I finally decided to use a revolver. All these questions occurred to me only in a shadowy and unreal fashion. I had only one fixed idea and that was that I could not go on living, for I sensed through the icy shell of my decision the horror of the life that would have been mine. It gazed at me hideously through vacant eyes and it seemed much more ugly and terrifying than the dark and quite unemotional conception I had of death.

In the afternoon, two days later, I was ready with my preparations. I still wanted to have a walk through the town. I had to take a couple of books back to the library. It was a comfort to me to know that in the evening I would no longer be alive. I felt like a man who has had an accident and is still partly under anesthetic and does not feel the pain, but has a foretaste of excruciating torture. He only hopes that he will sink into complete oblivion before the suspected pain becomes real. That is how I felt. I suffered less from an actual pain than from an agonizing fear that I might return to consciousness and have to empty the whole glass that death, which called me, was to take away from me. That was why I hurried through my walk, attended to what was necessary and went straight back. I made just a short detour in order not to go past Gertrude's house, for I felt, without being able to analyze it, that if I saw the house, the intolerable pain from which I was seeking escape would overwhelm and prostrate me.

So, breathing a sigh of relief, I went back to the house in which I lived, opened the gate and went immediately up the stairs, feeling lighter of heart. If the grief was still pursuing me and stretching out its claws toward me, if somewhere within me the frightful pain should begin to gnaw again, there were only a few stairs and seconds between me and liberation.

A man in uniform came down the stairs toward me. I moved aside and hastened to pass him, fearing I might be stopped. He then touched his cap and pronounced my name. I looked at him in dismay. Being addressed and stopped, which I had feared, caused me to tremble. Suddenly a feeling of exhaustion overpowered me. I felt that I was going to fall and there would be no hope of making the few necessary paces to reach my room.

Meanwhile, I stared in distress at the stranger. As the feeling of weakness grew, I sat down on one of the stairs. The man asked me if I was ill and I shook my head. He was holding something in his hand which he wanted to give me and which I would not take, until he almost forced it into my hand. I made a gesture of refusal and said: "I don't want it."

He called for the landlady but she was not there. He then took me by the arm in order to help me up. As soon as I saw that there was no escape and that he would not leave me alone, I suddenly pulled myself together. I stood up and walked toward my room, and he followed me. As I felt that he looked at me suspiciously, I pointed to my injured leg and pretended it was hurting me, and he believed me. I took out my purse and gave him a coin. He thanked me and finally pushed into my hand the thing that I knew I did not want to take. It was a telegram.

Wearily, I stood by the table. Someone had now stopped me and broken the spell. What was it? A telegram. From whom? It was all the same to me. It was irritating to receive a telegram just now. I had made all my preparations and at the last moment someone sends me a telegram. I looked around. A letter lay on the table.

I put the letter in my pocket; it did not tempt me. But I was intrigued by the telegram. I could not get it out of my thoughts and it disturbed me. I sat down and looked at it on the table and wondered whether to read it or not. It was, of course, an attack on my freedom; of that I had no doubt. Someone wanted to try to stop me, begrudged me my flight, wanted me to accept my sorrow and taste it to the full without being spared any twinge, stab or spasm of pain.

Why the telegram caused me so much anxiety, I do not know. I sat at the table a long time and did not dare to open it, feeling that it concealed some power that would draw me back and compel me to bear the unbearable from which I wanted to escape. When I finally did open it, my hand shook. I could only decipher the telegram slowly, as if I were translating the contents from an unfamiliar foreign language. It read: "Father dying. Please come at once. Mother."

I gradually realized what it meant. Only yesterday I had thought about my parents and regretted that I should have to give them pain, and yet it had only been a superficial consideration. Now they created obstacles, dragged me back and made claims upon me. I immediately thought of the conversations I had had with my father at Christmas. Young people, he had said, with their egotism and feeling of independence, can be brought to the point of ending their lives on account of an unfulfilled wish, but when one's life is bound up with those of others, one does not consider one's own desires to the same degree. And I was also tied by such a bond! My father was dying. My mother was alone with him and called me. The thought of his dying and her need for me did not at the moment affect me so deeply. I thought I knew of even greater griefs, but I fully realized that I could not now give them an extra burden to bear, ignore my mother's request and run away from them.

In the evening I was at the railway station ready for my journey, and automatically yet consciously did what was necessary. I obtained my ticket, put the change in my pocket, went on to the platform and entered the train. I sat in a corner of a compartment, prepared for a long night journey. A young man entered the compartment, looked around, greeted me and sat down opposite me. He asked me something, but I just looked at him, only wishing that he would leave me alone. He coughed and stood up, picked up his yellow leather traveling bag and left to look for another seat.

The train traveled through the night in blind, senseless haste, just as insensate and conscientious as I, as though there were something that would be missed or saved. Some hours later, when I put my hand in my pocket, I felt the letter. That is still there, I thought, and I opened it.

My publisher had written to me about concerts and fees, and he informed me that my affairs were going well and improving. A well-known critic had written about me and he congratulated me on it. Enclosed with the letter was a newspaper article with my name as the heading, and a long discourse on the position of present-day music and of Wagner and Brahms; then there was a review of my string music and songs, with high praise and good wishes. As I read the small black letters, I gradually realized that it was about me, that fame and the world were holding out their hands to me. For a moment I had to laugh.

The letter and the article had loosened the bandage from my eyes, and unexpectedly I looked back into the world and saw that I was not beaten and finished but that I was in the middle of it and belonged to it. I had to go on living as well as I could. Was it possible? Then everything about the past five days came back to me and all that I had felt as if in a stupor, and from which I had hoped to escape — it was all horrible, bitter and humiliating. It was all a death sentence that I had not executed, and I must leave my task undone.

I heard the train rattling along. I opened the window, and as we flew past I saw the gloomy stretches of country, dismal-looking bare trees with black branches, large farmhouses and distant hills. They all seemed unwilling to exist, to express sorrow and resentment. Some people might think all this was beautiful, but to me it only seemed sad. I recalled the song "Is that God's will?"

However much I tried to look at the trees and fields and roofs outside, however earnestly I tried to concentrate my thoughts on remote subjects and on anything I could think of without distress, I was unable to do so for long. I could not even think about my father; he had become remote with the trees and the countryside at night, and against my will and despite my efforts, my thoughts drifted back to forbidden things. I saw a garden with old trees in it, and among them a house with palm trees at the entrance, and inside on all the walls there were old, dark paintings. I went in and walked up the stairs past all the old pictures and no one saw me. I walked through like a ghost. There was a slim lady there with dark hair, who turned her back on me. I saw the man too and they embraced. I saw my friend Heinrich Muoth smile sadly and dejectedly, as he did sometimes, as if he already knew that he would abuse and ill-treat this fair lady too, and that there was nothing that could be done about it. It was stupid and senseless that this unhappy man, this reprobate, should attract the most charming women, and that all my love and good intentions should be in vain.

Awakening from a sleep or doze, I saw the gray of morning and a pale light in the sky through the window. I stretched out my stiff limbs and felt sad and sober; the course that lay before me seemed gloomy and vexatious. First of all I now had to think of my father and mother.

It was still gray and early morning when we approached the bridges and houses of my home town. In the smell and noise of the railway station I felt so weary and exasperated that I did not want to leave the train. However, I picked up my luggage and climbed into the nearest cab, which first traveled over smooth asphalt, then over slightly frosty ground, then crunched along a rough track and stopped at the large gate of our house, which I had never seen closed.

But now it was closed and when, dismayed and frightened, I pulled the bell, no one came and there was no response. I looked up at the house and felt as if I were having an unpleasant wild dream. The driver looked on in surprise and waited. Feeling wretched, I went to the other door, which was seldom used and which I had not gone through for years. This was open. When I went in, I found my father's office staff sitting there wearing gray coats as usual, and they were quiet and subdued. They rose at my entrance, for I was my father's heir. Klemm, the bookkeeper, who did not look any different than he had twenty years before, gave a short bow and looked at me inquiringly with a sad expression on his face.

"Why is the front door locked?" I asked.

"There is no one there."

"Where is my father?"

"In the hospital. You mother is also there."

"Is he still alive?"

"He was still alive this morning, but they think . . ."

"Tell me what has happened."

"Oh, of course, you don't know! It is still his foot. We all say he had wrong treatment for it. Suddenly he had severe pains and screamed terribly. Then he was taken to the hospital. Now he is suffering from blood poisoning. Yesterday at half past two we sent you a telegram."

"I see. Thank you. Could you please have a sandwich and a glass of wine brought to me quickly and order a cab for me."

My wishes were whispered to someone and then there was silence again. Someone gave me a plate and a glass. I ate a sandwich, drank a glass of wine, went out and climbed into a cab; a horse snorted, and soon we stood at the hospital gate. Nurses with white caps on their heads, and attendants wearing blue-striped linen suits passed along the corridors. Someone took me by the hand and led me into a room. Looking around, I saw my mother nod to me with tears in her eyes, and in a low, iron bed lay my father, changed and shrunken, his short gray beard standing out oddly.

He was still alive. He opened his eyes and recognized me despite his fever.

"Still composing music?" he asked quietly, and his voice and glance were kind as well as mocking. He gave me a wink which expressed a tired, ironic wisdom that had nothing more to impart, and I felt that he looked into my heart and saw and knew everything.

"Father," I said, but he only smiled, glanced at me again half mockingly, though already with a somewhat distracted look, and closed his eyes.

"You look terrible!" said my mother, putting her arm around me. "Was it such a shock?"

I could not say anything. Just then a young doctor came in, followed by an older one. The dying man was given morphine, and the clever eyes that had looked so understanding and ominiscient a moment ago did not open again. We sat beside him and watched him lying there; we saw his face change and become peaceful, and we waited for the end. He lived for several hours and died late in the afternoon. I could feel nothing but a dull sorrow and extreme weariness. I sat with tear-stained eyes and toward evening fell asleep sitting by the deathbed.

Chapter Six

That life is difficult, I have often bitterly realized. I now had further cause for serious reflection. Right up to the present I have never lost the feeling of contradiction that lies behind all knowledge. My life has been miserable and difficult, and yet to others, and sometimes to myself, it has seemed rich and wonderful. Man's life seems to me like a long, weary night that would be intolerable if there were not occasionally flashes of light, the sudden brightness of which is so comforting and wonderful that the moments of their appearance cancel out and justify the years of darkness.

The gloom, the comfortless darkness,

lies in the inevitable course of our daily lives. Why does one repeatedly rise in the morning, eat, drink, and go to bed again? The child, the savage, the healthy young person does not suffer as a result of this cycle of senseless automatic activities. If a man does not think too much, he rejoices at rising in the morning, and at eating and drinking. He finds satisfaction in them and does not want them to be otherwise. But if he ceases to take things for granted, he seeks eagerly and hopefully during the course of the day for moments of real life, the radiance of which makes him rejoice and obliterates the awareness of time and all thoughts on the meaning and purpose of everything. One can call these moments creative, because they seem to give a feeling of union with the creator, and while they last, one is sensible of everything being necessary, even what is seemingly fortuitous. It is what the mystics call union with God. Perhaps it is the excessive radiance of these moments that makes everything else appear so dark, perhaps it is the feeling of liberation, the enchanting lightness and the suspended bliss that make the rest of life seem so difficult, cloying and oppressive. I do not know. I have not traveled very far in thought and philosophy.

However, I do know that if there is a state of bliss and a paradise, it must be an uninterrupted sequence of such moments, and if this state of bliss can be attained through suffering and dwelling in pain, then no sorrow or pain can be so great that one should seek escape from it.

A few days after my father's funeral — I was still in a state of bewilderment and mental exhaustion — I found myself walking aimlessly in a suburban street. The small, attractive houses awakened vague memories in me, until I recognized the house and garden of my old teacher, who had tried to convert me to the faith of the theosophists some years ago. I knocked at the door and he appeared, recognized me and led me in a friendly manner into his study, where the pleasant smell of tobacco smoke hovered around his books and plants.

"How are you?" asked Mr. Lohe. "Oh, of course, you have just lost your father. You look wretched. Has it affected you so deeply?"

"No," I said. "My father's death would have affected me more deeply if I had still been on cool terms with him, but during my last visit I drew closer to him and rid myself of the painful feeling of guilt that one has toward good parents from whom one receives more love than one can give."

"I am glad about that."

"How are you going on with your theosophy? I should like you to talk to me, because I am unhappy."

"What is wrong?"

"Everything. I can't live and I can't die. Everything seems meaningless and stupid."

Mr. Lohe puckered up his kind, peaceful-looking face. I must confess that even his kind, rather plump face had put me in a bad humor, and I did not expect to obtain any kind of comfort from him and his wisdom. I only wanted to hear him talk, to prove his wisdom of no avail and to annoy him because of his happy state and optimistic beliefs. I was not feeling amicably disposed toward him or anyone else.

But the man was not as self-satisfied and absorbed in his doctrines as I had thought. He looked at me with real concern and sadly shook his fair head.

"You are ill, my dear fellow," he said firmly. "Perhaps it is only physical, and if so, you can soon find a remedy. You must then go into the country, work hard and not eat any meat. But I don't think it is that. You are mentally sick."

"Do you think so?"

"Yes. You are suffering from a sickness, one that is fashionable, unfortunately, and that one comes across every day among sensitive people. It is related to moral insanity and can also be called individualism or imaginary loneliness. Modern books are full of it. It has insinuated itself into your imagination; you are isolated; no one troubles about you and no one understands you. Am I right?"

"Almost," I admitted with surprise.

"Listen. Those who suffer from this illness need only a couple of disappointments to make them believe that there is no link between them and other people, that all people go about in a state of complete loneliness, that they never really understand each other, share anything or have anything in common. It also happens that people who suffer from this sickness become arrogant and regard all other healthy people who can understand and love each other as flocks of sheep. If this sickness were general, the human race would die out, but it is only found among the upper classes in Central Europe. It can be cured in young people and it is, indeed, part of the inevitable period of development."

His ironic professor's tone of voice annoyed me a little. As he did not see me smile or look as if I was going to defend myself, the kind, concerned expression returned to his face.

"Forgive me," he said kindly. "You are suffering from the sickness itself, not the popular caricature of it. But there really is a cure for it. It is pure fiction that there is no bridge between one person and another, that everyone goes about lonely and misunderstood. On the contrary. What people have in common with each other is much more and of greater importance than what each person has in his own nature, what makes him different from others."

"That is possible," I said. "But what good does it do me to know all this? I am not a philosopher and I am not unhappy because I cannot find truth. I only want to live a little more easily and contentedly."

"Well, just try! There is no need for you to study any books or theories. But as long as you are ill, you must believe in a doctor. Will you do that?"

"I will try."

"Good! If you were physically ill and a doctor advised you to take baths or drink medicine or go to the seaside, you might not understand why this or that remedy should help, but you would try it and obey his instructions. Now do the same with what I advise you. Learn to think more about others than yourself for a time. It is the only way for you to get better."

"How can I do that? Everyone thinks about himself first."

"You must overcome that. You must cultivate a certain indifference toward your own well-being. Learn to think, *what can I do*? There is only one expedient. You must learn to love someone so much that his or her well-being is more important than your own. I don't mean that you should fall in love. That would give the opposite result!"

"I understand, but with whom shall I try it?"

"Begin with someone close to you, a friend or a relation. There is your mother. She has had a great loss; she is now alone and needs someone to comfort her. Look after her and try to be of some help to her."

"My mother and I don't understand each other very well. It will be difficult."

"If your good intentions stop short, it will indeed be difficult. It's the old story of not being understood! You don't always want to be thinking that this or that person does not fully understand you and is perhaps not quite fair to you. Try yourself to understand other people, try to please them and be just to them. You do that and begin with your mother. Look, you must say to yourself: Life does not give me much pleasure in any case, so why shouldn't I try it this way for once? You have lost interest in your own life, so don't give it much thought. Give yourself a task, inconvenience yourself a little."

"I will try. You are right. It is all the same to me whatever I do. Why shouldn't I do what you advise me."

What impressed me about his remarks was the similarity between them and the views on life that my father had expounded at our last meeting: "Live for others! Don't take yourself so seriously!" This outlook was quite at variance with my feelings. It also had a flavor of the catechism and confirmation instruction which, like every healthy young person, I thought of with aversion and dislike. Yet it was really not a question of opinions and a philosophy of life but a practical attempt to make my unhappy life tolerable. I would try it.

I looked with surprise at this man, whom I had never taken quite seriously and whom I was now permitting to act as my adviser and doctor. But he really seemed to show toward me some of that love which he recommended. He seemed to share my suffering and sincerely to wish me well. In any case, I felt that I had to take some drastic measure to continue living and breathing like other people. I had thought of a long period of solitude among the mountains or of losing myself in hard work, but instead I would obey my friendly adviser, as I had no more faith in my experience and wisdom.

When I told my mother that I did not intend to leave her by herself and hoped she would turn to me and share her life with me, she shook her head sadly.

"What are you thinking of?" she protested gently. "It would not be so easy. I have my own way of life and could not make a fresh start. In any case, you ought not to be burdened with me. You ought to be free."

"We could try it," I said. "It may be more successful than you think."

At the beginning I had enough to do to prevent me from brooding and giving way to despair. There was the house and an extensive business, with assets in our favor and bills to be paid; there were books and accounts, money loaned and money received, and it was a problem to know what was to become of all these things. At the beginning I naturally wanted to sell everything, but that could not be done so quickly. My mother was attached to the old house, my father's will had to be executed and there were many difficulties. It was necessary for the bookkeeper and a notary to assist. The days and weeks passed by with arrangements, correspondence about money and debts, and plans and disappointments. Soon I could not cope with all the accounts and official forms. I engaged a solicitor to help the notary and left them to disentangle everything.

In this process my mother did not always receive what was her due. I tried to make things as easy as possible for her during this period. I relieved her of all business matters, I read to her and took her for drives. Sometimes I felt an urge to tear myself away and leave everything, but a sense of shame and a certain curiosity as to how it would turn out prevented me from doing so.

My mother thought of nothing but the deceased, and showed her grief in small feminine acts that seemed strange and often trivial to me. At the beginning I had to sit in my father's place at the table; then she considered it unfitting and the place had to remain empty. Sometimes I could not talk to her enough about my father; at other times she became quiet and looked at me sadly as soon as I mentioned his name. Most of all, I missed my music. At times I would have given much to be able to play my violin for an hour, but only after many weeks had passed did I venture to do so and even then she sighed and seemed offended. She appeared to be little

224

interested in my joyless efforts to draw closer to her and win her friendship.

This often made me suffer and made me want to give up my attempts, but I continued to persevere and grew accustomed to the succession of cheerless days. My own life lay broken and dead. Only occasionally did I hear a dim echo of the past when I heard Gertrude's voice in a dream, or when melodies from my opera suddenly came back to me during a quiet hour. When I made a journey to R. to give up my rooms there and to collect my possessions, everything connected with the place seemed extremely remote. I only visited Teiser, who had been so loyal to me. I did not venture to inquire about Gertrude.

I gradually began to fight a secret battle against my mother's reserved and resigned behavior, which for a long time distressed me extremely. I often asked her to tell me what she would like and whether I displeased her in any way. She would then stroke my hand and with a sad smile would say: "Don't worry, my child. I am just an old woman." I then began to make investigations elsewhere and did not disdain to make inquiries of the bookkeeper and the servants.

I discovered many things. The chief one was this: my mother had one close relation and friend in the town; she was an unmarried cousin. She did not go about a great deal but she was very friendly with my mother. This Miss Schniebel had not liked my father much and she had a real dislike for me, so she had not been to our house recently. My mother had once promised Miss Schniebel she could come and live with her if she outlived my father, and this hope appeared to have been shattered by my presence. When I gradually learned all this, I visited the old lady and tried to make myself as agreeable as possible to her. Being involved in eccentricities and little intrigues was new to me and I almost enjoyed it. I managed to persuade the lady to come to our house again, and I perceived that my mother was grateful to me for this. To be sure, they now both tried to dissuade me from selling the house, as I had wished, and they were successful in doing so. Then the lady tried to usurp my place in the house and obtain the long-desired place of my father, from which I barred her with my presence. There was room for both of us, but she did not want a master in the house and refused to come and live with us. On the other hand, she visited us frequently, made herself indispensable as a friend in many small things, treated me diplomatically, as though I were a dangerous power, and acquired the position of an adviser in the household, which I could not contest with her.

My poor mother did not take either her part or mine. She was weary and suffered a great deal as a result of the change in her life. Only gradually did I realize how much she missed my father. On one occasion, on going into a room in which I did not expect to see her, I found her occupied at a wardrobe. It startled her when I came in, and I went out quickly. I had noticed, however, that she had been handling my father's clothes, and when I saw her later, her eyes were red.

In the summer a new battle commenced. I wanted to go away with my mother. We both needed a holiday, and I also hoped it would cheer her up and draw her closer to me. She showed little interest at the thought of traveling, but raised no objection. On the other hand, Miss Schniebel was very much in favor of my mother remaining and my going alone, but I had no intention of giving way in this matter. I expected to gain a great deal from this holiday. I was beginning to feel ill at ease in the old house with my restless, sorrowful mother. I hoped to be of more help to her away from the place, and also hoped to control my own thoughts and moods better.

So I arranged that we should set off on our journey at the end of June. We moved on day by day; we visited Constance and Zürich and traveled over the Brünig Pass to the Bernese Oberland. My mother remained quiet and listless, bore patiently with the journey and looked unhappy. At Interlaken she complained that she could not sleep, but I persuaded her to come on to Grindelwald, where I hoped we should both feel at peace. During this long, senseless, joyless journey, I realized the impossibility of running away and escaping from my own misery. We saw beautiful green lakes reflecting magnificent old towns, we saw mountains which appeared blue and white, and bluish-green glaciers glistening in the sunlight, but we viewed everything unmoved and without pleasure. We felt ashamed, but we were only depressed and weary of everything. We went for walks, looked up at the mountains, breathed the pure, sweet air, heard the cowbells ringing in the meadows, and said, "Isn't it lovely?" but dared not look each other in the face.

We endured it for a week at Grindelwald. Then one morning my mother said: "It is no use; let us go back. I should like to be able to sleep again at night. If I become ill and die, I want to be at home."

So I quietly packed our trunks, silently agreeing with her, and we traveled back quicker than we had come. But I felt as if I were not going back home, but to a prison, and my mother also displayed little satisfaction.

On the evening of our return home, I said to her: "How would you feel if I now went off alone? I should like to go to R. I would willingly remain with you if it served any purpose, but we both feel ill and miserable and only have a bad effect on each other. Ask your friend to come and live with you. She can comfort you better than I."

She took my hand and stroked it gently as was her wont. She nodded and smiled at me, and her smile distinctly said: "Yes, go by all means!"

Despite all my efforts and good intentions, the only results were that we had harassed each other for a couple of months and she was more estranged from me than ever. Although we had lived together, each of us had borne his own burden, not sharing it with the other, and had sunk deeper into his own grief and sickness. My attempts had been in vain and the best thing for me to do was to go and leave the way open for Miss Schniebel.

I did this without delay, and not knowing where else to go, I went back to R. On my departure it occurred to me that I no longer had a home. The town in which I was born, in which I had spent my youth and had buried my father, did not matter to me any more. It had no more ties for me and had nothing to give me but memories. I did not tell Mr. Lohe on taking my leave from him, but his advice had not helped.

By chance, my old rooms in R. were still vacant. It seemed like a sign to me that it is useless to try to break off associations with the past and escape from one's destiny. I again lived in the same house and rooms in the same town. I unpacked my violin and my work, and found everything as it had been, except that Muoth had gone to Munich and he and Gertrude were engaged to be married.

I picked up the parts of my opera as if

they were the ruins of my previous life from which I still wished to try to build something, but the music returned very slowly to my benumbed soul and only really burst forth when the writer of all my texts sent me the words for a new song. It arrived at a time when the old restlessness frequently returned to me, and with feelings of shame and a thousand misgivings I would walk around outside the Imthors' garden. The words of the song were:

> *The south wind roars at night,*
> *Curlews hasten in their flight,*
> *The air is damp and warm.*
> *Desire to sleep has vanished now,*
> *Spring has arrived in the night*
> *In the wake of the storm.*
>
> *I, too, at night no longer sleep,*
> *My heart feels young and strong.*
> *Memory takes me by the hand*
>   *to peep*
> *Again at days of joy and song,*
> *But frightened at so bold a deed*
> *It does not linger long.*

Be still, my heart, away with pain!
Though passion stirs again
In blood that now flows slowly
And leads to paths once known,
These paths you tread in vain
For youth has flown.

These verses affected me deeply and reawakened life and music in me. Reopened and smarting severely, the long-concealed wound was converted into rhythms and sounds. I composed the music to this song and then picked up the lost threads of my opera, and after my long spell of inaction I again plunged deeply into the swift creative current with feverish intoxication, until I finally emerged to the free heights of feeling, where pain and bliss are no longer separate from each other and all passion and strength in the soul press upward in one steady flame.

On the day that I wrote my new song and showed it to Teiser, I walked home in the evening past an avenue of chestnut trees, with a feeling of renewed strength for work. The past months still gazed at me as if through masked eyes, and appeared empty and without comfort, but my heart now beat more quickly and I no longer conceived why I should want to escape from my sorrow. Gertrude's image arose clearly and splendidly from the dust. I looked into her bright eyes without fear and left my heart unprotected to receive fresh pain. It was better to suffer because of her and to thrust the thorn deeper into the wound than to live far away from her and to waste away far from her and my real life. Between the dark, heavily laden treetops of the spreading chestnut trees could be seen the dark blue of the sky, full of stars, all solemn and golden, which extended their radiance unconcernedly into the distance. That was the nature of the stars. And the trees bore their buds and blossoms and scars for everyone to see, and whether it signified pleasure or pain, they accepted the strong will to live. Flies that lived only for a day swarmed toward their death. Every life had its radiance and beauty. I had insight into it all for a moment, understood it and found it good, and also found my life and sorrows good.

I finished my opera in the autumn. During this time I met Mr. Imthor at a concert. He greeted me warmly and was rather surprised that I had not let him know that I was in town. He had heard that my father had died and that since then I had been living at home.

"How is Miss Gertrude?" I asked as calmy as possible.

"Oh, you must come and see for yourself. She is going to be married in November, and we are counting on you to be there."

"Thank you, Mr. Imthor. And how is Muoth?"

"He is well. You know, I am not too happy about the marriage. I have long wanted to ask you about Mr. Muoth. As far as I know him, I have no complaints to make, but I have heard so many things about him. His name is mentioned in connection with different women. Can you tell me anything about it?"

"No, Mr. Imthor. It would serve no

purpose. Your daughter would hardly change her mind because of rumors. Mr. Muoth is my friend and I wish him well if he finds happiness."

"Very well. Will you be coming to see us soon?"

"I think so. Goodbye, Mr. Imthor."

It was not long before that I would have done everything to place obstacles between the two of them, not because of envy or in the hope that Gertrude would still be drawn toward me, but because I was convinced and felt in advance that things would not go well with them, because I was aware of Muoth's self-tormenting melancholy and excitability and of Gertrude's sensitiveness, and because Marian and Lottie were so vivid in my memory.

Now I thought differently. The shattering of my whole life, half a year of loneliness, and the realization that I was leaving my youth behind me had changed me. I was now of the opinion that it was foolish and dangerous to stretch out one's hand to alter other people's destinies. I also had no reason to think that my hand was skillful or that I could regard myself as one who could help and understand other people, after my attempts in this direction had failed and discouraged me. Even now I strongly doubt the ability of people to alter and shape their own lives and those of other people to any appreciable extent. One can acquire money, fame and distinction, but one cannot create happiness or unhappiness, not for oneself or for others. One can only accept what comes, although one can, to be sure, accept it in entirely different ways. As far as I was concerned, I would make no more strenuous endeavors to try and find a place in the sun but would accept what was allotted to me, try to make the best of it and, if possible, turn it into some good.

Although life continues independent of such reflections, sincere thoughts and resolutions leave the soul more at peace and help one to bear the unalterable. At least, it subsequently appeared to me that since I had become resigned and indifferent toward my personal fate, life had treated me more gently.

That one sometimes unexpectedly achieves without effort what one has previously been unable to attain, despite all endeavors and good will, I soon learned through my mother. I wrote to her every month, but had not heard from her for some time. If there had been anything wrong, I should have learned about it, so I did not give her much thought and continued to write my letters, brief notes as to how things were going for me, in which I always included kind regards to Miss Schniebel.

These greetings were recently no longer delivered. The two women had done as they desired but their friendship had not survived the fulfillment of their wishes. Improved conditions had inflated Miss Schniebel's ego. Immediately after my departure she triumphantly occupied the seat of conquest and settled down in our house. She now shared the house with her old friend and cousin and, after long years of want, regarded it as a well-deserved turn of luck to be able to reign and give herself airs as one of the mistresses of a dignified household. She did not acquire expensive habits or prove wasteful — she had been in straitened circumstances and semi-poverty too long to do that. She neither wore more expensive clothes nor slept between finer linen sheets. On the contrary, she really began to scrimp and collect only now that it was worthwhile and there was something to save — but she would not renounce authority and power. The two maids had to obey her no less than my mother, and she also dealt with servants, workmen and postmen in an imperious manner. And very gradually, since passions are not extinguished by their fulfillment, she also extended her domineering sway over things that my mother would not so readily concede. She wanted my mother's visitors to be her visitors too and would not suffer my mother to receive anyone except in her presence. She did not want only to hear extracts from letters that were received, particularly those from me, but wanted to read the letters herself. Finally, she formed the opinion that many things in my mother's house were not looked after and conducted as she thought they ought to be. Above all, she considered that the discipline of the domestic servants was not strict enough. If a maid went out in the evening, or talked too long to the postman, or if the cook asked for a free Sunday, she strongly reproved my mother for her leniency and delivered long lectures to her on the correct way to conduct a household. Furthermore, it hurt her very much to see how often her rules of economy were grossly ignored. Too much coal was ordered, and too many eggs were unaccounted for by the cook! She bitterly opposed things of that nature, and that was how discord arose between the friends.

Until then my mother had taken the line of least resistance although she did not agree with everything, and was in many ways disappointed with her friend, whose relationship toward her she had imagined to be different. Now, on the other hand, when old respected customs in the house were in danger, when her everyday comforts and the peace of the house were at stake, she could not refrain from objecting and putting up some resistance, which, however, she could not do as forcefully as her friend. There were differences of opinion and little arguments in a friendly way, but when the cook gave notice — and it was only with difficulty, after many promises and almost apologies, that my mother persuaded her to stay — the question of authority in the house began to lead to a real battle.

Miss Schniebel, proud of her knowledge, experience, thrift and organizing abilities, could not understand why all these qualities were not appreciated, and she felt justified in criticizing the previous household economy, in finding fault with my mother's housekeeping and in showing her disdain for the customs and traditions of the house. Then my mother mentioned my father, under whose management everything in the house had gone so well for many years. He had not tolerated trivialities and petty economies; he had given the servants freedom and privileges; he had hated disputes with the maids and incidents of a disagreeable nature. But when my mother mentioned my father whom she had previously criticized occasionally, but who since his death had become holy to her, Miss Schniebel could no longer contain herself and reminded my mother pointedly how she had often expressed her opinion about the deceased; it was high time to abandon the old ways and let reason reign. Out of consideration for her friend, Miss Schniebel had not wanted to spoil her memory of the deceased, but now that he had been mentioned, she had to confess that many things which were unsatisfactory in the house were due to the old master, and she did not see why, now that my mother was free, things should continue in the same way.

That was a blow which my mother could never forgive her cousin. Previously it had been a need and pleasure to grumble to her confidential friend and find fault with the master of the house; now she would not suffer the slightest shadow to be cast upon his sacred memory. She began to feel that the incipient revolution in the house was not only disturbing but, above all, a sin against the deceased.

This state of affairs continued without my knowledge. When for the first time my mother mentioned in a letter this lack of harmony, even though she did so carefully and discreetly, it made me laugh. In my next letter I omitted greetings to the spinster but did not refer to my mother's allusions. I thought that the women would settle the affair better without me. Besides, there was another matter which was occupying my mind much more.

October had arrived and the thought of Gertrude's forthcoming marriage was constantly on my mind. I had not been to her house again and had not seen her. After the wedding, when she would be away, I thought of making contact with her father again. I also hoped that in time a good, friendly relationship would be established between Gertrude and me. We had been too close to each other to be able to cancel out the past so easily, but I did not yet have the courage for a meeting which, knowing her, she would not have tried to avoid.

One day someone knocked at my door in a familiar way. Full of misgivings, I jumped up and opened it. Heinrich Muoth stood there and held out his hand to me.

"Muoth!" I cried, and gripped his hand tightly, but I could not look into his eyes without everything coming back to me and hurting me. I again saw the letter lying on his table, the letter in Gertrude's handwriting, and saw myself taking leave from her and wanting to die. Now he stood there looking at me keenly. He seemed a little thinner but as handsome and proud as ever.

"I did not expect you," I said quietly.

"Didn't you? I know that you do not go to Gertrude's house any more. As far as I am concerned — let us not talk about it! I have come to see how you are and also how your work is progressing. How is the opera going?"

"It is finished. But first of all, how is Gertrude?"

"She is well. We are being married soon."

"I know."

"Well, aren't you going to visit her sometime soon?"

"Later. I first want to see if things go well for her in your hands."

"Hm . . ."

"Heinrich, forgive me, but sometimes I cannot help thinking about Lottie, whom you treated so badly."

"Forget about Lottie. It served her right. No woman is beaten if she doesn't want to be."

"Oh! About the opera, I don't really know where I should submit it first. It would have to be a good theater, although I don't know, of course, whether it will be accepted."

"Oh, yes, it will. I wanted to talk to you about that. Bring it to Munich. It will most likely be accepted there; people are taking an interest in you. If necessary, I will risk my job for you. I don't want anyone else to sing my part before I do."

That was very helpful. I gladly agreed and promised to arrange for copies to be made as soon as possible. We discussed details and continued to talk with some embarrassment, as if it were a matter of life and death to us, and yet we only wanted to pass the time and close our eyes to the chasm that had appeared between us.

Muoth was the first to bridge the gap.

"Do you remember the first time you took me to the Imthors?" he said. "It is a year ago now."

"I know," I said. "You don't need to remind me. It would be better if you went now!"

"No, not yet, my friend. So you still remember. Well, if you were in love with the girl then, why didn't you say: 'Leave her alone, leave her for me!' It would have been enough. I would have understood the hint."

"I couldn't do that."

"You couldn't? Why not? Who told you to look on and say nothing until it was too late?"

"I did not know whether she cared for me or not. And then — if she prefers you, I can't do anything about it."

"You are a child! She might have been happier with you. Every man has the right to woo a woman. If you had only said a word to me at the beginning, if you had just given me a hint, I should have kept away. Afterwards, it was naturally too late."

This conversation was painful to me.

"I think differently about it," I said, "but you need not worry. Now leave me in peace! Give her my regards and I will come and visit you in Munich."

"Won't you come to the wedding?"

"No, Muoth, that would be in bad taste. But — are you being married in church?"

"Yes, of course, at the church."

"I am glad about that. I have composed something for the occasion, an organ piece. Don't worry, it is quite short."

"You are a good fellow! It's hell for me to bring you so much bad luck!"

"I think you should say 'good luck,' Muoth."

"Well, we won't quarrel. I must go now; there are still things to buy and goodness knows what to do. You will send the opera soon, won't you? Send it to me and I will take it to the right people myself. And before the wedding the two of us must spend an evening together. Perhaps tomorrow! Yes? Well, goodbye."

So I was drawn into the old circle again and passed the night with thoughts and sorrows that had recurred a hundred times. The following day I visited an organist whom I knew and asked him to play my music at Muoth's wedding. In the afternoon I went through my overture with Teiser for the last time, and in the evening I went to the inn where Heinrich was staying.

I found a room prepared for us with an open fire and candles. There was a white cloth on the table with flowers and silver plate. Muoth was already there waiting for me.

"Now, my friend, this is a farewell

celebration, more for me than for you. Gertrude sends her regards. Today we shall drink to her health."

We filled our glasses and silently emptied the contents.

"Now let us think only about ourselves. Youth is slipping away, my dear friend, don't you feel it also? It should be the best time of one's life. I hope that is false, like all these well-known sayings. The best should still lie ahead, otherwise the whole of life isn't worthwhile. When your opera is produced, we'll talk again."

We relaxed and drank some heavy Rhine wine. Afterwards, we sank back into the easy chairs with cigars and champagne, and for an hour it reminded us both of old times when we used to take pleasure in discussing plans and chatting lightly. We looked at each other pensively but frankly and felt happy to be in each other's company. At times like these, Heinrich was kinder and more gracious than usual. He knew how fleeting these pleasures were and clung to them fondly as long as his mood endured. Quietly, with a smile, he talked to me about Munich, told me little incidents about the theater, and practiced his old art of describing people and situations in a few concise words.

After he had sketched his conductor, his future father-in-law and others amusingly and clearly but without malice, I drank to his health and said: "What about me? Can you describe people of my type, too?"

"Oh, yes," he said calmly with a nod and gazed at me with his dark eyes. "You are the artist type in every way. The artist is not, as ordinary people think, a gay sort of person who flings off works of art here and there out of sheer exuberance. Unfortunately he is usually a poor soul who is being suffocated with surplus riches and therefore has to give some of them away. It is a fallacy that there are happy artists; that is just philistines' talk. Lighthearted Mozart kept up his spirits with champagne and was consequently short of bread, and why Beethoven did not commit suicide in his youth instead of composing all that wonderful music, no one knows. A real artist has to be unhappy. Whenever he is hungry and opens his bag, there are only pearls inside it."

"But if he desires a little pleasure and warmth and sympathy in life, a dozen operas and trios and things like that don't help him much."

"I suppose not. An hour like this with a glass of wine and a friend, if he has one, and a pleasant chat about this remarkable life is about the best thing he can expect. That's how it is, and we should be glad to have that at least. Just think how long it takes a poor devil to make a good sky-rocket, and the pleasure it gives scarcely lasts a minute! In the same way, one has to conserve joy and peace of mind and a good conscience to enrich a pleasant hour here and there. Good health, my friend!"

I did not at all agree with his philosophy, but what did it matter? I was glad to spend an evening like this with the friend I feared I was going to lose and who was equally uncertain about me, and I meditated upon the past that still lay so close to me and yet encircled my youth with its carefree days that would return no more.

Eventually the evening came to an end and Muoth offered to walk home with me, but I told him not to trouble. I knew that he did not like walking with me outside; my slow, halting walk irritated him and made him bad-tempered. He did not like being inconvenienced and little things like that are often the most annoying.

I was pleased with my organ piece. It was a kind of prelude, and for me it was a detachment from the past, thanks and good wishes to the betrothed couple and an echo of happy times spent with both of them.

On the day of the wedding I went to the church early and, concealed by the organ, looked down at the ceremony. When the organist began to play my music, Gertrude looked up and smiled at her fiancé. I had not seen her all this time and she looked even taller and slimmer than usual in her white dress. Gracefully, with a serious expression on her face, she walked along the narrow, adorned path to the altar by the side of the proud-looking, erect man. It would not have made such a splendid picture if instead of him, I, a cripple with a crooked leg, had walked along this solemn path.

Chapter Seven

It was ordained that I should not dwell for long on my friends' wedding and that my reflections, desires and self-torture should not be directed along this channel.

I had given little thought to my mother during this time. I knew, indeed, from her last letter that the peace and comfort of the house was not all that it might be, but I had neither reason nor desire to interfere in the strife between the two ladies and accepted it, just a little maliciously, as one of those things in which my judgment was unnecessary. Since then I had written to her without receiving any reply. I had enough to do with the provision and examination of copies of my opera without thinking about Miss Schniebel.

Then I received a letter from my mother which surprised me by its unusual bulk alone. It was a letter of distress, complaining of her companion, whose transgressions in the house and against my mother's peace of mind I now learned about in detail. She found it hard to write to me about the matter but did so with dignity and discretion. It was simply a confession of the disillusionment she had suffered in connection with her old friend and cousin.

Now my mother not only completely understood why my late father and I disliked Miss Schniebel, but she was agreeable to the sale of the house if I still wished it; she would go and live somewhere else, if only to escape from this Schniebel woman.

"It might be a good thing for you to come here. Lucie, of course, already knows what I am thinking and planning — she is very sharp — but relations are too strained for me to be able to tell her what I have to say without offending her. She ignores my hints that I would prefer to be alone in the house again and that I could manage without her, and I do not want an open quarrel. I know that she would reproach me and put up a strong resistance if I asked her outright to leave. It would therefore be better if you would come and deal with the matter. I do not want any unpleasantness and I do not want her to be put to any expense, but she must clearly and definitely be told to go."

I would even have been prepared to *slay* the dragon if my mother had desired it. With great amusement I made preparations for the journey and set off for home. As soon as I entered the old house, I was aware of the invasion of a new spirit. The large, comfortable sitting room, in particular, had assumed a gloomy, cheerless and impoverished appearance. Everything looked carefully guarded and tended to. There were so-called "runners" on the old solid floor, long, dark strips made from cheap, ugly material, to protect the floorboards and save cleaning. The old piano that had stood unused in the drawing room for years was also enveloped in a protective cover, and although my mother had tea and cakes ready for me and had tried to make things look as pleasant as possible, there was such an atmosphere of old maid's meticulousness and naphthalene about the place that as soon as I came in I smiled at my mother and wrinkled up my nose. She understood immediately.

I had hardly sat down when the dragon came in, trotted along the runners toward me and did me the honor of asking at great length how I was getting on. I inquired in detail as to how she was keeping and apologized for the old house that did not perhaps offer every comfort to which she was accustomed. Taking the lead in the conversation away from my mother, she adopted the role of mistress of the house, saw to the tea, eagerly replied to my polite remarks and seemed rather flattered, but also uneasy and distrustful, by my excessive friendliness. Her suspicions were aroused but she had no option but to accept my courtesies and respond with her own store of somewhat antiquated polite phrases. Displaying apparent mutual devotion and esteem, we went on throughout the evening. We heartily wished each other a good night's sleep and left each other like diplomats of the old school. Yet, despite the sweetmeat, I think the demon did not sleep much that night, while I rested contentedly, and my poor mother, after perhaps many nights passed in a state of annoyance and depression, again slept for the first time with a feeling of being the sole mistress in her own house.

At breakfast the following morning, we began the same polite game. My mother, who had only listened quietly and intently the previous evening, now participated with enjoyment, and we overwhelmed Schniebel with polite phrases that drove her into a corner and even made her sad, for she realized quite well that these fine phrases did not come from my mother's heart. I almost felt sorry for the old maid as she became anxious, tried to humble herself and praised everything, but I thought of the dismissed housemaid, of the discontented-looking cook who had only remained for my mother's sake. I thought of the covered piano and the whole wretched atmosphere in my father's hitherto pleasant house, and I remained adamant.

After the meal I told my mother to go and lie down a little, and I remained alone with her cousin.

"Are you accustomed to having a nap after a meal?" I inquired politely. "If so, don't let me disturb you. I wanted to talk to you about something, but it is not so urgent."

"Oh, please go on. I never sleep during the day. Thank goodness I am not so old yet. I am quite at your service."

"Thank you very much, Miss Schniebel. I wanted to express my gratitude to you for the kindness you have shown toward my mother. She would have been very lonely without you in this large house. However, things are going to be changed now."

"What!" she cried, rising to her feet.

"How are things going to be changed?"

"Don't you know yet? My mother has at last decided to fulfill my wish for her to come and live with me. Naturally we cannot leave the old house empty, so it will soon be put up for sale."

The lady gazed at me disconcertedly.

"Yes, I am sorry too," I continued regretfully. "This has been a very tiring time for you. You have taken such a kind and practical interest in the house that I cannot thank you enough."

"But what shall I — where shall I—?"

"Oh, we shall find a solution to that. You will of course have to look for somewhere else to live, but there is no great hurry. You will be glad yourself to take things easier."

She had remained standing. She was still polite but her tone of voice had become considerably sharper.

"I don't know what to say," she cried bitterly. "Your mother, sir, promised to let me live here; it was a permanent arrangement. Now, after I have taken an interest in the house and helped your mother with everything, I am turned out into the street."

She began to sob and wanted to run away, but I took hold of her thin hand and pressed her back into the easy chair.

"It is not as bad as all that," I said, smiling. "It does alter circumstances a little that my mother wants to move from here. However, the sale of the house was not decided by her, but by me, as I am the owner. My mother will see to it that you are not pressed in your search for a new home and she will make the necessary arrangements for it herself. You will thus be more comfortable than you were previously and you will still, so to speak, be a guest of hers."

Then came the expected reproaches, arrogance, weeping, alternate pleading and boasting, but in the end the sullen woman realized that the wisest thing to do was to accept the situation. She then withdrew to her room and did not even appear for coffee.

My mother thought we ought to send it up to her room, but I wanted to have my revenge after all this polite play and let Miss Schniebel stay there in her mood of independence until the evening, when, although quiet and sulky, she punctually appeared for dinner.

"Unfortunately, I have to go back to R. tomorrow," I said during the meal, "but if you should need me for anything, Mother, I could always come again quickly."

As I said this, I did not look at her but at her cousin, and she realized what I meant. My parting from her was brief but almost cordial.

"My dear," said my mother later, "you settled that very well. Thank you very much. Won't you play me something from your opera?"

That was something I left undone for the time being, but a barrier had been broken down and a new relationship began to be established between the old lady and me. That was the best that had come out of the business. She now had confidence in me and I was pleased at the thought of setting up a small household with her after my long spell of being homeless. I left my kind regards to Miss Schniebel and departed with a feeling of contentment. Shortly after my return, I began to look around here and there, wherever there were small, attractive houses to let. Teiser helped me in this respect, and his sister usually came along, too. They both rejoiced with me and hoped that the two small families would live happily near each other.

In the meantime, I had sent the score of my opera to Munich. Two months later, shortly after my mother's arrival, Muoth wrote to me that it had been accepted but that it could not be rehearsed that season. It would, however, be performed at the beginning of the next winter. So I had good news to tell my mother. When Teiser heard about it, he danced for joy and arranged a celebration.

My mother wept when we moved into our attractive little house, and said it was not good to be transplanted in one's old age, but I thought it was a very good move, as did the Teisers, and it pleased me to see how much Brigitte helped my mother. The girl had few acquaintances in the town and while her brother was at the theater she often felt lonely at home, although she did not admit it. Now she often came to see us and not only helped us to get organized and settle in but also helped my mother and me along the difficult path of living together harmoniously. She knew how to make it apparent to the old lady when I had the need to be quiet and alone; she was often at hand to help me out. She also pointed out to me many of my mother's needs and wishes which I had never guessed at and of which my mother had never told me. So we soon settled down in our peaceful little home, which was different and more modest than my previous conception of a home, but which was good and pleasant enough for one who had not progressed any further than I had.

My mother now became familiar with some of my music. She did not like every piece and withheld comment about most of them, but she saw and believed that it was not just a sport and a pastime but demanding work that was to be taken seriously. Above all, she was surprised to find that the musician's life, which she had considered to be very capricious, was hardly less strenuous than the business life that my late father had led. We now found it easier to talk about him and gradually I heard numerous tales about them both, about my grandparents and about my own childhood. I enjoyed hearing about the past and the family, and I no longer felt as if I did not belong. On the other hand, my mother learned to let me go on my own way and to have confidence in me, even when I locked myself in my room during working hours, or when I was irritable. She had been very happy with my father and this had made her trials and tribulations with the Schniebel woman all the harder to bear. She now gained confidence again and gradually stopped talking about becoming old and lonely.

In the midst of all this comfort and modest happiness, the feeling of grief and dissatisfaction with which I had lived so long became submerged. It did not sink to unfathomable depths but lingered deep down in my soul. It confronted me on many a night and maintained its rights. The more remote the past seemed, the more was I aware that my love and my sorrow were ever with me as a quiet reminder. Occasionally, in the past, I had thought I was in love. When I was still a youth, infatuated with pretty, carefree Liddy, I thought I knew about love; then again, when I first saw Gertrude and felt that she was the answer to my questions and obscure wishes, when the pain began and passion and unknown depths succeeded friendship and understanding, and finally when she was lost to me, I thought I knew what love was. My love for her had persisted and was always with me and I knew that I would never desire another woman or wish to kiss another woman's lips, for Gertrude had won my heart.

Her father, whom I visited from time to time, now seemed to know about my feelings toward her. He asked me for the music of the prelude I had written for her wedding and displayed a quiet good will toward me. He must have sensed how glad I was to have news of her and how reluctant I was to ask, and he passed on to me much of the contents of her letters. They often had something in them about me, particularly in regard to the opera. She wrote that a good singer had been found for the soprano part, and how pleased she would be to hear this much beloved work in its entirety at last. She was also glad that I now had my mother with me. I did not know what she wrote about Muoth.

My life proceeded peacefully; the undercurrents no longer forced their way to the surface. I was working on a Mass and had ideas for an oratorio, for which I still needed the text. When I was obliged to think about the opera, it was like an alien world to me. My music was developing along other lines; it was becoming more simple and more peaceful; its aim was to soothe, not to excite.

During this time the Teisers were a great comfort to me. We saw each other almost every day. We read, made music, went for walks together and joined each other on free days and outings. Only in the summer, when I did not wish to hinder these strenuous walkers, did we part for a few weeks. The Teisers again wandered around the Tirol and Voralberg, and sent me small boxes of edelweiss. I, however, took my mother to relatives in North Germany, whom she visted every year. I settled down by the shore of the North Sea. There, day and night, I heard the old song of the sea and in the sharp, fresh air it accompanied my thoughts and melodies. From here I had the courage to write to Gertrude in Munich for the first time, not to Mrs. Muoth, but to my friend Gertrude whom I told about my music and my dreams. Perhaps it will give her pleasure, I thought, and a few kind words and a friendly greeting can do no harm. Against my own will I could not help but mistrust my friend Muoth, and I was always a little worried on Gertrude's account. I knew him too well, this self-willed melancholy man who was accustomed to giving way to his moods and never made sacrifices for anyone, who was carried away by powerful urges and who, in more thoughtful hours, saw his whole life as a tragedy. If it really was an illness to be lonely and misunderstood, as my good friend Mr. Lohe had declared, then Muoth suffered more from this illness than anyone else.

I had no news from him. He did not write. Even Gertrude sent me only a short note of thanks, asking me to come to Munich early in the autumn, as rehearsals for my opera would commence at the beginning of the season.

At the beginning of September, when we were all in town again and back to our everyday life, the Teisers came to my house one evening to have a look at the work I had done during the summer. The most important work was a short lyrical piece for two violins and the piano. We played it. Brigitte sat down at the piano; above my music I could see her head and her thick braided fair hair, the top of which gleamed like gold in the candlelight. Her brother stood beside me and played the first-violin part. It was simple, lyrical music which softly pined and faded away like a summer evening, neither happy nor sad, but hovering in the mood of a twilight that is ending, like a cloud aglow at sunset. The Teisers liked this short piece, particularly Brigitte. She rarely said anything about my music; she quietly maintained a kind of girlish awe toward me, regarding me with admiration, for she considered me to be a great maestro. This day she took courage and expressed her particular pleasure. She looked at me frankly with her light blue eyes and nodded so that the light glimmered on her blond braids. She was very pretty, almost beautiful.

In order to please her, I took her piano part and wrote a dedication in pencil above the music: "To my friend Brigitte Teiser," and handed it back to her.

"That will always be over this little piece now," I said gallantly and bowed. She read the dedication slowly and blushed. She held out her small strong hand to me and suddenly her eyes filled with tears.

"Are you serious?" she asked quietly.

"Oh, yes," I said, and laughed. "And I think this piece of music suits you very well, Miss Brigitte."

Her gaze, which was still veiled with tears, astonished me, it was so serious and ungirlish — but I did not pay further attention to the matter. Teiser now put his violin away, and my mother, who already knew what he liked, filled the glasses with wine. The conversation became lively. We argued about a new operetta which had been produced a few weeks earlier, and I only remembered the little incident with Brigitte later in the evening, when they both departed and she again looked at me strangely.

In the meantime, rehearsals of my opera had commenced in Munich. As one of the principal parts was in Muoth's good hands and Gertrude had praised the soprano, the orchestra and the chorus became my chief concern. I left my mother in the care of my friends and traveled to Munich.

The morning after my arrival I walked

along the attractive broad streets to Schwabing and to the quietly situated house where Muoth lived. I had almost completely forgotten about the opera. I only thought about him and Gertrude and how I would find them. The cab stopped at an almost rural byroad in front of a small house that stood among autumnal-looking trees. Yellow maple leaves lay on both sides of the road, swept into heaps.

With some trepidation I went in. The house gave me the impression of being comfortable and prosperous. A servant took my coat.

In the large room into which I was led I recognized two large old paintings that had been brought from the Imthors' house. On one wall there was a new portrait of Muoth that had been painted in Munich, and while I was looking at it Gertrude came in.

My heart beat quickly at seeing her again after such a long time. She had changed into a more serious, mature woman, but she smiled at me in the old friendly way and held out her hand to me.

"How are you?" she asked in a friendly manner. "You have grown older but you look well. We have expected you for a long time."

She inquired about all her friends, about her father and my mother, and as she became interested and overcame her first shyness, I regarded her in the same light as I had in the past. Suddenly my embarrassment disappeared and I talked to her as to a good friend, told her how I spent the summer by the sea, about my work, the Teisers, and finally even about poor Miss Schniebel.

"And now," she exclaimed, "your opera is going to be performed! You will be very pleased about it."

"Yes," I said, "but I am even more pleased at the thought of hearing you sing again."

She smiled. "I shall be pleased, too. I sing quite often, but almost always for myself alone. I shall sing all your songs. I have them here and I do not let the dust settle on them. Stay for a meal with us. My husband will be coming soon and he can go along with you to see the conductor in the afternoon."

We went into the music room and she sang my songs. I became quiet and found it difficult to remain calm. Her voice had become more mature and sounded more confident, but it soared as easily as ever and transported me in my memory to the best days of my lifen so that I looked at the piano keys as if bewitched, quietly played the well-known notes and, listening with closed eyes, could not for moments distinguish between the present and the past. Did she not belong to me and my life? Were we not as near to each other as brother and sister, and very close friends? To be sure, she would have sung differently with Muoth!

We sat chatting for a while, feeling happy and not having much to say to each other, for we knew that no explanations were necessary between us. How things were with her and what relations were like between her and her husband, I did not think about then. I would be able to observe that later. In any event, she had not swerved from her

274

path and become untrue to her nature, and if she had a load to bear, she certainly bore it with dignity and without bitterness.

An hour later Heinrich, who had heard that I had arrived, came in. He immediately began to talk about the opera, which seemed more important to everyone else than it did to me. I asked him how he was and how he liked being in Munich.

"Like everywhere else," he said seriously. "The public does not like me because it feels that I do not care about it. I am hardly ever favorably received at my first entrance. I always have to hold people first and then carry them away with me. I thus succeed without being popular. Sometimes I also sing badly, I must admit that myself. Well, your opera will be a success — you can count on that — for you and for me. Today we shall go and see the conductor; tomorrow we shall invite the soprano to come and see us and whoever else you wish to meet. Tomorrow morning there is an orchestral rehearsal. I think you will be satisfied."

During lunch I observed that he was exceptionally polite toward Gertrude, which made me suspicious. It was like that the whole time I was in Munich, and I saw them both every day. They were an extremely handsome couple and made an impression wherever they went. Yet they were cool toward each other, and I thought that only Gertrude's strength of character and superior nature made it possible for her to mask this coolness with a polite and dignified veneer. It appeared as if she had not long before awakened from her passion for this handsome man and still hoped to recover her inward stillness. In any event, she acted in accordance with good form. She was too well bred and fine a person to play the part of the disillusioned and misunderstood woman before friends or to show her secret sorrow to anyone, even if she could not hide it from me. But she could also not have endured any look or gesture of understanding or sympathy from me. We spoke and acted all the time as if there were no cloud over her marriage.

How long this state of affairs would be maintained was uncertain and depended on Muoth, whose incalculable nature I saw kept under restraint by a woman for the first time. I was sorry for both of them but I was not very surprised to find this situation. They had both enjoyed their passion; now they had to learn resignation and preserve this happy time in their memory or they must learn to find their way to a new kind of happiness and love. Perhaps a child would bring them together again, not back to the abandoned Paradise garden of love's ardor, but to a new will to live together and to draw closer to each other. Gertrude had the strength and serenity of character for it, I knew. I did not dare to think whether Heinrich had the same capacity. However sorry I was that the fierce storm of their first passion and pleasure in each other had already passed, I was pleased at the way both of them behaved, preserving their dignity and respect not only in front of people but also in each other's company.

Meanwhile, I did not accept the

invitation to stay at Muoth's house, and he did not press me. I went there every day and it gladdened me to see that Gertrude liked me to come and enjoyed chatting and making music with me, so that the pleasure was not only mine.

It was now definite that my opera would be performed in December. I stayed in Munich two weeks, was present at all the orchestral rehearsals, made alterations and adjustments here and there, but saw the work in good hands. It seemed strange to see the singers, the violinists and flautists, the conductor and the chorus occupied with my work, which had now become alien to me and had life and breath that were no longer mine.

"Just wait," said Heinrich Muoth. "You will soon have to breathe the accursed air of publicity. I almost wish for your sake that the opera will not be a success, for you will then have the mob after you. Then you will have to deal with locks of hair and autographs, and taste the approbation and kindness of the admiring public. Everyone is already talking about your crippled leg. Anything like that makes one popular!"

After the necessary rehearsals I took my departure, arranging to come back a few days before the performance. Teiser asked me endless questions about the rehearsals. He thought of numerous orchestral details that I had scarcely considered and he was more excited and anxious about the whole affair then I was. When I invited him and his sister to come with me to the performance, he jumped for joy. On the other hand, my mother did not welcome the winter journey and all the excitement, and I agreed that she should stay behind. Gradually, I began to feel more excited and had to take a glass of port at night to help me sleep.

Winter came early, and our little house and garden lay deep in snow when, one morning, the Teisers called for me in a cab. My mother waved goodbye to us from the window, the cab drove off, and Teiser, with a thick scarf round his neck, sang a traveling song. During the whole long journey he was like a boy going home for the Christmas holidays, and pretty Brigitte was glowing, expressing her pleasure more quietly. I was glad of their company, for I was no longer calm, and awaited the events of the next few days like one under sentence.

Muoth, who was waiting for me at the railway station, noticed it immediately. "You are suffering from stage fright, young man," he said and laughed with pleasure. "Thank goodness for that! After all, you are a musician and not a philosopher."

He seemed to be right, for my excitement lasted until the performance took place, and I did not sleep during those nights. Muoth was the only calm person among us all. Teiser burned with excitement; he came to every rehearsal and made endless criticisms. Huddled up and attentive, he sat beside me during rehearsals, beat time with his clenched hand during difficult passages, and alternately praised or shook his head.

"There's a flute missing!" he cried out at the first orchestral rehearsal he attended, so loudly that the conductor looked across at us with annoyance.

"We have had to omit it," I said, smiling.

"Omit a flute? Why? What a crazy thing to do! Be careful, or they will ruin the whole overture."

I had to laugh and hold him back forcibly because he was so critical. But during his favorite part, where the violas and cellos came in, he leaned back with closed eyes, pressed my hand from time to time, and afterward whispered to me, abashed: "That almost brought tears to my eyes. It is beautiful!"

I had not yet heard the soprano part sung. It now seemed strange and sad to hear it sung for the first time by another singer. She sang it well, and I thanked her as soon as she had finished, but inwardly I thought of the afternoons when Gertrude had sung those words, and I had a feeling of unadmitted discontent, as when one gives a precious possession away and sees it in strange hands for the first time.

I saw little of Gertrude during those days. She observed my excitement with a smile and let me alone. I had visited her with the Teisers. She received Brigitte very warmly, and the girl was full of admiration for the beautiful, gracious woman. From that time she was most enthusiastic about Gertrude and praised her volubly, and her brother did likewise.

I can no longer remember the details of the two days preceding the performance; everything is confused in my mind. There were additional reasons for excitement: one singer became hoarse, another was annoyed at not having a larger part and behaved very badly during the last rehearsals. The conductor became cooler and more formal as a result of my directions. Muoth came to my aid at opportune moments, smiled calmly at all the tumult, and during this time was of more value to me than Teiser, who ran here and there like a demon, making criticisms everywhere. Brigitte looked at me with reverence but also with some sympathy when, during quieter periods, we sat together in the hotel, weary and rather silent.

The days passed and the evening of the performance arrived. While the audience was entering the theater, I stood backstage without having anything more to do or to suggest. Finally, I stayed with Muoth, who was already in his costume and in a small room away from all the noise was slowly emptying half a bottle of champagne.

"Will you have a glass?" he asked sympathetically.

"No," I said. "Doesn't it overexcite you?"

"What? All the activity outside? It is always like that."

"I mean the champagne."

"Oh no, it soothes me. I always have to have a glass or two before I want to do anything. But go now, it is nearly time."

I was led by an attendant into a private box, where I found Gertrude and both the Teisers, as well as an important personage from the management of the theater, who greeted me with a smile.

Directly afterward we heard the second bell. Gertrude gave me a friendly look and nodded to me. Teiser, who sat behind me, seized my arm and pinched it with excitement. The theater became dark, and the sounds of my overture solemnly rose to me from below. I now became calmer.

Then my work appeared before me, so familiar and yet so alien, which no longer needed me and had a life of its own. The pleasures and troubles of past days, the hopes and sleepless nights, the passion and longing of that period confronted me, detached and transformed. Emotions experienced in secret were transmitted clearly and movingly to a thousand unknown people in the theater. Muoth appeared and began singing with some reserve. Then his voice grew stronger; he let himself go and sang in his deeply passionate manner; the soprano responded in a high, sweet voice. Then came a part which I could so well remember hearing Gertrude sing, which expressed my admiration for her and was a quiet confession of my love. I averted my glance and looked into her bright eyes, which acknowledged me and greeted me warmly, and for a moment the memory of my whole youth was like the sweet fragrance of a ripe fruit.

From that moment I felt more calm and listened like any other member of the audience. There was a burst of applause. The singers appeared before the curtain and bowed. Muoth was recalled a number of times and smiled calmly down into the now illuminated theater. I was also pressed to appear, but I was far too overcome by emotion and had no desire to limp out of my pleasant retreat.

Teiser, on the other hand, laughed with a face like the rising sun, put his arm through mine and also impetuously shook both hands of the important personage from the theater management.

The banquet was ready and would have been held even if the opera had been a failure. We traveled to the banquet in cabs, Gertrude with her husband, and the Teisers and I together. During the short journey

Brigitte, who had not yet said a word, suddenly began to weep. At first she tried to restrain herself, but she soon covered her face with her hands and let the tears flow. I did not like to say anything and was surprised that Teiser was likewise silent and asked no questions. He just put his arm around her and murmured a few kind, comforting words as one would to a child.

Later, during the shaking of hands, the good wishes and toasts, Muoth winked at me sarcastically. People inquired with interest about my next work and were disappointed when I said that it would be an oratorio. Then they drank to my next opera, which has never been written to this day.

Only much later in the evening, when we had departed and were on our way to bed, was I able to ask Teiser what was the matter with his sister, why she had wept. She herself had long since gone to bed. My friend looked at me searchingly and with some surprise, shook his head and whistled, until I repeated my question.

"You are as blind as a bat," he then

said reproachfully. "Have you not noticed anything then?"

"'No," I said with a growing suspicion of the truth.

"Well, I will tell you. The girl has been fond of you for a long time. Naturally she has never told me so, any more than she has you, but I have noticed it, and to tell the truth, I should be very happy if something came of it."

"Oh dear!" I said with real sadness. "But what was the matter this evening?"

"You mean, why did she weep? You are a child! Do you think we did not see?"

"See what?"

"Good heavens! You don't need to tell me anything, and you were right to be silent about it in the past; but then you should not have looked at Mrs. Muoth like that. Now we understand quite clearly."

I did not ask him to keep my secret. I knew I could trust him. He gently placed his hand on my shoulder.

"I can now well imagine, my dear friend, all that you have gone through during these years without telling us anything. I once had a similar experience myself. Let us stay together now and make good music, shall we? And also see that the girl is consoled. Give me your hand! It has been wonderful! Well, goodbye until I see you again at home. I am traveling back with Brigitte tomorrow morning."

We then parted, but he came running back a few moments later and said with great seriousness: "The flute must be included again in the next performance. Don't forget!"

That was how the day of rejoicing ended, and we all lay awake for a long time thinking about it. I thought about Brigitte, too. I had seen a great deal of her all this time and I was a good friend of hers, which was all I desired, just as Gertrude had been a good friend of mine, and when Brigitte had guessed my love for another, it was the same for her as it was for me when I had discovered the letter at Muoth's house and had later loaded my revolver. Although this made me feel sad, I could not help but smile.

I spent most of the remainder of my days in Munich with the Muoths. It was no longer like those afternoons in the past when the three of us first used to sing and play together, but in the afterglow of the performance of the opera there was an unspoken mutual remembrance of that time, and also an occasional rekindling of former feelings between Muoth and Gertrude. When I finally said goodbye to them, I gazed back for a while at the peaceful-looking house among the bare trees. I hoped to return there some day and would gladly have given my little success and happiness away in order to help those two inside to draw close to each other again and for always.

Chapter Eight

On my return home I was greeted, as Heinrich had predicted, with the notoriety of my success and many of its unpleasant but, in part, slightly ridiculous consequences. It was easy to dispose of the burden of commercial matters; I simply put the opera in the hands of an agent. But there were visitors, newpaper people, publishers and foolish letters, and it took time to grow accustomed to the smaller burdens of sudden fame and to recover from initial disillusionment. People have a peculiar way of claiming a hold on a well-known name, with no distinction made among infant prodigies, composers, poets, thieves and murderers. One person wants a photograph, another an autograph, a third begs for money; every young colleague submits his work, asks for an opinion and is extremely flattering, but if one does not reply, or really tells him what one thinks, the admirer suddenly turns bitter, uncivil and vengeful. Magazines want the famous man's picture, newspapers describe his life, origins and appearance; school friends remind him of their existence, and distant relatives declare they said years ago their cousin would become famous one day.

Among the harassing letters of this kind, there was one from Miss Schniebel that amused me. There was also one from someone I had not thought about for a long time: the fair Liddy, who wrote without mentioning our toboggan ride, and in the tone of an old faithful friend. She had married a music teacher in her home town and gave me her address so that I could soon send all my compositions with a flattering dedication to her. She enclosed a photograph, however, that showed the well-known features grown older and coarsened. I replied to her in very cordial terms.

But these little things concerned minor issues that left no important trace behind. Even the good and refreshing fruits of my success, such as making the acquaintance of cultured and distinguished people who had music in their souls and did not just talk about it, did not belong to my real life, which later, as in the past, remained detached and has changed very little since then. All that remains is for me to tell you of the turn of events in the lives of my closest friends.

Old Mr. Imthor did not entertain as much as when Gertrude had been there, but every three weeks, among the numerous pictures at his house, he held a musical evening with selected chamber music, which I regularly attended. I sometimes brought Teiser along with me, but Imthor pressed me to come and see him apart from these visits. So I sometimes went there in the evening, which was his favorite time, and kept him company in his simply furnished study, where there was a portrait of Gertrude on one of the walls. The old gentleman and I, although outwardly reserved with each other, gradually came to a good understanding and felt the need to talk to each other, and it was therefore not rare for us to talk about what occupied our minds most. I had to tell him about Munich and I did not conceal the impression I had received of the relationship between the couple. He nodded understandingly.

"Everything may yet turn out all right," he said, sighing, "but we can't do anything. I am looking forward to the summer, when I shall have my child with me for two months. I rarely visit Munich and do not care to go there. Besides, she behaves so bravely that I do not want to disturb her and make her weaken."

Gertrude's letters did not bring anything new. But when she visited her father round Easter, and also came to our little house, she looked thin and tense, and although she tried to be natural with us and to cover things up, we often saw an expression of unaccustomed hopelessness on her face, which had become serious. I played my latest music to her, but when I asked her to sing something for us, she gently shook her head and refused.

"Another time," she said uncertainly.

We could all see that she was unhappy, and her father confessed to me later that he had suggested she remain with him for good, but she had refused.

"She loves him," I said.

He shrugged his shoulders and looked at me with distress. "I don't know. Who can analyze this misery? But she said she was staying with him for his sake. He is so bewildered and unhappy and needs her more than he thinks. He does not say anything to her, but it is written on his face."

Then the old man lowered his voice and said quite softly and with shame: "She means he drinks."

"He has always done that a little," I said, trying to comfort him, "but I have never seen him drunk. He keeps himself under control in that way. He is a nervous type of person who is not used to self-discipline, but perhaps causes himself more suffering than he does other people."

None of us knew how terribly these two fine people suffered in secret. I do not think that they ever stopped loving each other, but deep down in their natures they did not belong to one another; they only drew closer through passion and in the intoxication of exalted hours. A calm acceptance of life and a tacit understanding of his own nature were things that Muoth had never known and Gertrude could only be patient with and regret his outbursts and depressions, his swift change of moods, his continual desire for self-forgetfulness and intoxication; but she could not change or live with them. So they loved each other and yet were never quite close to each other, and while he saw himself cheated of all his hopes of finding peace and happiness through her, Gertrtude realized, and suffered in this knowledge, that all her good intentions and efforts were in vain, and that she could not comfort him and save him from himself. Thus they both had their secret dream and dearest wish shattered. They could only remain together by making sacrifices and showing forbearance, and it was brave of them to do this.

I saw Heinrich again in the summer when he brought Gertrude to her father. He was more gentle and attentive to her and to me than I had ever seen him before. I perceived how much he feared to lose her, and I also felt that he would never be able to bear such a loss. But she was weary and desired nothing but rest and quiet in order to compose herself and recover her strength and tranquillity. We spent one mild evening together in our garden. Gertrude sat between Brigitte and my mother, whose hand she held. Heinrich walked quietly to and fro among the roses, and I played a violin sonata with Teiser on the terrace. The way Gertrude rested there and enjoyed the peace of those hours, how Brigitte affectionately pressed close to the sad, beautiful woman, and how Muoth walked about quietly in the shadows with his head bowed and listened for us, are things that are indelibly stamped on my mind. Afterwards Heinrich said somewhat jokingly but with sad eyes: "Just look at the three women sitting there together; the only one among them who looks happy is your mother. We should also try to grow old like her."

After this, we all parted ways. Muoth traveled alone to Bayreuth, Gertrude went with her father into the mountains, the Teisers to Steiermark, and my mother and I went to the coast of the North Sea again. There I often walked along the shore, listened to the sea, and thought as I had done in my youth, with amazement and horror, about the sad and senseless confusion of life, that one could love in vain, that people who meant well toward each other should work out their destinies separately, each one going his own inexplicable way, and how each would like to help and draw close to the other and yet was unable to do so, as in troubled meaningless dreams. I often thought of Muoth's remarks about youth and old age, and I was curious whether life would ever seem simple and clear to me. My mother smiled when I mentioned this during conversation and looked really peaceful. She made me feel ashamed by reminding me of my friend Teiser, who was not yet old but was old enough to have had his share of experiences, and yet went on living in a carefree way like a child, with a Mozart melody on his lips. It had nothing to do with age, I saw that clearly, and perhaps our suffering and ignorance was only the sickness about which Mr. Lohe had talked to me. Or was that wise man another child like Teiser?

However it may be, thinking and brooding did not change anything. When music stirred my being, I understood everything without the aid of words. I was then aware of pure harmony in the essence of life and felt that there must be a meaning and a just law behind everything that happened. Even if this was an illusion, it helped me to live and was a comfort to me.

Perhaps it would have been better if

Gertrude had not parted from her husband for the summer. She had begun to recover, and when I saw her again in the autumn, after my journey, she looked much better and capable of managing again. But the hopes we had built on this improvement were destined for disappointment.

Gertrude had felt better while staying with her father for a few months. She had been able to indulge in her need for rest, and with a feeling of relief could remain in this quiet state without a daily battle, just as a tired person yields to sleep when left alone. It appeared, however, that she was more exhausted than we had thought and that she herself knew, for now that Muoth was to come for her soon, she became dispirited again, did not sleep, and entreated her father to let her stay with him a little longer.

Imthor was naturally rather alarmed at this, as he thought she would be glad to return to Muoth with renewed strength and determination, but he did not argue with her and even cautiously suggested a longer separation for the time being, with a view to a divorce later. She protested against this with great agitation.

"But I love him," she cried vehemently, "and I will never be disloyal to him. Only it is so difficult to live with him! I just want to rest a little longer, perhaps another couple of months, until I feel stronger."

Mr. Imthor tried to comfort her. He himself had no objection to having his child with him a little longer. He wrote to Muoth telling him that Gertrude was still not well and wished to remain with him for some time yet. Unfortunately, Muoth did not receive this news well. During the time they had been separated, his longing for his wife had become very great. He had looked forward to seeing her again and was full of good resolutions for completely regaining her love.

Imthor's letter came as a great disappointment to him. He immediately wrote an angry letter full of suspicions about his father-in-law. He felt that the latter had influenced her against him as he desired a dissolution of the marriage. He demanded an immediate meeting with Gertrude, whom he hoped to win over again. Mr. Imthor came to me with the letter and for a long time we considered what should be done. We both thought it would be best for a meeting between the couple to be avoided at the moment, as Gertrude obviously could not stand any outbursts of emotion. Imthor was very concerned and asked me if I would go to see Muoth and persuade him to leave Gertrude in peace for a while. I know now that I should have done that. At the time I had some misgivings and thought it would be unwise to let my friend know that I was his father-in-law's confidant and acquainted with things in his life that he himself did not wish to disclose to me. So I declined, and all that transpired was that Mr. Imthor wrote another letter, which of course did not help matters.

Finally, Muoth arrived without warning and alarmed us all with the scarcely restrained vehemence of his love and suspicions. Gertrude, who did not know about the short exchange of letters, was quite astonished and confused by his unexpected appearance and his almost violent emotions. There was a painful scene, the details of which I did not learn. I only know that Muoth urged Gertrude to return with him to Munich. She declared she was ready to do as he wished, if there was no alternative, but asked to be allowed to remain with her father a little longer, as she was weary and still needed rest. He then accused her of wanting to forsake him and insinuated that she had been instigated by her father to do so. He became even more suspicious when she gently tried to explain, and in a fit of anger and bitterness he was so foolish as to command her abruptly to return to him. Her pride then asserted itself. She remained calm but refused to listen to him further and declared that she would now remain with her father in any event. The morning following this scene, Muoth tried to conciliate her, and ashamed and repentant, he now granted all her wishes. He then traveled back to

Munich without coming to see me.

I was alarmed when I heard about it and saw the trouble lying ahead which I had feared from the beginning. After that ugly and foolish scene, I thought, it might now be a long time before she would feel calm and strong anough to return to him, and meanwhile there was a danger of his becoming reckless, and despite all his longings, he might become even more estranged from her. He would not long be able to endure being alone in the house in which he had been happy for a time. He would give way to despair, drink and perhaps go with other women who still ran after him.

In the meantime, all was quiet. He wrote to Gertrude and again asked her forgiveness. She answered his letter and in a sympathetic and friendly manner urged him to be patient. I saw little of her at this time. Occasionally I tried to persuade her to sing, but she always shook her head. Yet several times I found her at the piano.

It seemed strange to me to see this

beautiful, proud woman, who had always been so strong, cheerful and serene, now timid and shaken to her very being. She sometimes came to see my mother, inquired how we were keeping, sat beside the old lady on the gray settee for a short time, and made an attempt to chat with her. It grieved me to hear her and to see how difficult she found it to smile. Appearances were kept up as if neither I nor anyone else knew of her sorrow, or regarded it as a nervous state and physical weakness. So I could hardly look into her eyes, in which her unconfessed grief, about which I was not supposed to know, was so clearly written. We talked and lived and met as if everything was the same as it had always been, and yet we felt uncomfortable in each other's presence and avoided each other. In the midst of this sad confusion of feelings, I was now and then seized by the notion, causing me sudden excitement, that her heart no longer belonged to her husband and that she was free, and it was now up to me not to lose her again, but to win her for myself and shelter her by my side from all storms and sorrows. I then locked myself in my room, played the passionate and yearning music of my opera, which I suddenly loved and understood again, lay awake at nights full of longing, and again suffered all the former laughable torments of youth and unfulfilled desires, no less intensely than in the past when I had first desired her and given her that single, unforgettable kiss. I felt it burn on my lips again and in a few hours it destroyed the peace and resignation of years.

Only in Gertrude's presence did my passion subside. Even if I had been foolish and ignoble enough to pursue my desires and, without consideration for her husband, who was my friend, had tried to win her heart, I should have been ashamed to show anything but sympathy and consideration when faced by this sad, gentle woman, who was so completely wrapped up in her sorrow. The more she suffered and seemed to lose hope, the prouder and more unapproachable did she become. She held her fine dark head as erect and as proud as ever and did not allow any of us to make the slightest attempt to approach and help her.

These long weeks of ominous silence were perhaps the most difficult in my life. Here was Gertrude, close to me yet unapproachable, with no way for me to reach her, and wishing to remain alone; there was Brigitte, who I knew loved me and with whom, after I had avoided her for some time, a tolerable relationship was slowly being established. And among us all there was my old mother, who saw us suffering, who guessed everything but did not trust herself to say anything, as I myself maintained an obstinate silence and felt I could not tell her anything about my own state. But worst of all was the horror of being compelled to look on with the helpless conviction that my best friends were heading for disaster, without my being able to reveal that I knew the reaason why.

Gertrude's father seemed to suffer most of all. I had known him for years as a clever, vigorous, self-possessed man, but he had now aged and changed; he spoke more quietly and less calmly; he no longer joked, and looked worried and miserable. I went to see him one day in November, chiefly to hear any news and be cheered up myself rather than to comfort him.

He received me in his study, gave me one of his expensive cigars and began to talk to me in a light, polite manner. He did this with an effort and soon abandoned it. He looked at me with a troubled smile and said: "You want to know how things are, don't you? Very bad, my dear friend. The child has suffered more than we knew, otherwise she would have dealt with the situation better. I am in favor of a divorce but she will not hear of it. She loves him, at least she says so, and yet she is afraid of him. That is bad. The child is ill; she closes her eyes, will not listen to reason any more, and thinks everything will be all right if people will only wait and leave her in peace. That is just nerves, of course, but her illness seems to be more deeply rooted. Just think, she sometimes even fears that her husband might ill-treat her if she returns to him, and yet she professes to love him."

He did not seem to understand her and watched the course of events with a feeling of helplessness. To me, her sufferings were quite conceivably the result of conflict between love and pride. She was afraid not that he would beat her but that she would no longer respect him, and while anxiously temporizing, she hoped to regain her strength. She had been able to control and steady him but by doing this had so exhausted herself that she no longer had confidence in her powers; that was her illness. She longed for him and yet feared that she would lose him completely if a fresh attempt at a reconciliation did not prove successful. I now saw clearly how futile and illusory my bold speculations about winning her love had been.

Gertude loved her husband and would never care for anyone else.

Mr. Imthor avoided talking to me about Muoth, as he knew I was a friend of his, but he hated him and could not understand how he had been able to attract Gertrude. He regarded him as a kind of wicked sorcerer who captured innocent people and never released them. Passion is always a mystery and unaccountable, and unfortunately there is no doubt that life does not spare its purest children and often it is just the most deserving people who cannot help loving those who destroy them.

During this troubled state of affairs, I received a short letter from Muoth, which relieved the tension. He wrote:

Dear Kuhn,

Your opera will now be performed everywhere, perhaps better than here. However, I should be very glad if you would come down again, say next week, when I sing the role in your opera twice. You know that my wife is ill and I am here alone. You could thus stay with me without standing on ceremony.

Kind regards,
MUOTH

He wrote so few letters, and never any unnecessary ones, that I immediately decided to go. He must need me. For a moment I thought of telling Gertrude. Perhaps this was an opportunity to break down the barrier. Perhaps she would give me a letter to take to him, or pass on a kind message, ask him to come over or even come with me. It was just an idea, but I did not carry it out. I only visited her father before departing.

It was late autumn; the weather was wretched, wet and stormy. From Munich one could at times see for an hour the nearby mountains, which were covered with fresh snow. The town was gloomy and wet with rain. I traveled immediately to Muoth's house. Everything there was the same as it had been the year before, the same servant, the same rooms and the same arrangement of furniture, but the place looked uninhabited and empty; it also lacked the flowers that Gertrude had always arranged. Muoth was not in. The servant took me to my room and helped me to unpack. I changed my clothes, and as my host had not yet arrived, I went down into the music room, where I could hear the trees rustling behind the window and had time to think about the past. The longer I sat there looking at the pictures and turning the leaves of books, the sadder I became, as if this household was beyond help. I sat down impatiently by the piano in order to rid myself of these unprofitable thoughts, and I played the wedding prelude that I had composed, as if by doing so I could bring back the happiness of the past.

At last I heard quick, heavy footsteps close by and Heinrich Muoth came in. He held out his hand and looked at me wearily.

"Excuse me for being late," he said. "I was busy at the theater. You know that I am singing this evening. Shall we eat now?"

I followed him out of the room. I found him changed; he was absent-minded and apathetic. He only talked about the theater and seemed unwilling to discuss anything else. Only after the meal, when we sat facing each other in the yellow cane chairs, did he say unexpectedly: "It was very good of you to come. I will make a special effort this evening."

"Thank you," I said. "You don't look well."

"Don't I? Well — we shall soon cheer up. I am a grass-widower. You know that, don't you?"

"Yes."

He looked away. "Have you any news about Gertrude?"

"Nothing special. She is still in a nervous state and does not sleep well—"

"Oh well, let us not talk about it. She is in good hands."

He stood up and walked about the room. I felt that he still wanted to say something. He looked at me keenly and, I thought, distrustfully.

Then he laughed and left it unsaid. "Lottie has turned up again," he said, changing the subject.

"Lottie?"

"Yes, Lottie who once came to see you and told you a tale about me. She has married someone here, and it appears that she still takes an interest in me. She came to visit me here."

He looked at me again slyly and laughed when he saw that I was shocked.

"Did you receive her?" I asked with some hesitation.

"Oh, you think I am capable of it! No, my dear fellow, I had her sent away. But forgive me, I am talking nonsense. I am so terribly tired, and I have to sing this evening. If you don't mind, I will go and lie down for an hour and try to sleep."

"Certainly, Heinrich, have a good rest. I will go to town for a while. Will you order a cab for me?"

I could not sit in this house in silence again and listen to the wind in the trees. I traveled to town without any aim, and wandered into the old art museum. I looked at the pictures there for half an hour in the poor light. Then it was time to close and I could think of nothing better to do than read newpapers in a café and look through the large windowpanes on to the wet road. I resolved that I would break through this barrier of coolness at any cost and talk openly to Heinrich.

But when I returned, I found him smiling and in a good humor.

"I only needed a good sleep," he said cheerfully. "I feel quite revived now. You must play something for me! The prelude, if you will be so good."

Pleased and surprised to see such a sudden change in him, I did as he wished. When I had finished playing, he began to talk as he used to, ironically and somewhat skeptically. He let his imagination run riot and completely won my heart again. I thought of the early days of our friendship, and when we left the house in the evening I looked around involuntarily and said: "Don't you keep a dog now?"

"No — Gertrude did not like dogs."

We traveled to the theater in silence. I greeted the conductor and was shown to a seat. I again heard the well-known music, but everything was different from the last time. I sat alone in my box, Gertrude was absent, and the man who acted and sang down there was also changed. He sang with fervor and passion. The public seemed to like him in this role and followed it with enthusiasm from the beginning. But to me his fervor seemed excessive and his voice too loud, almost forced. During the first interval I went down to see him. He was back in his dressing room drinking champagne, and on exchanging a few words with him I saw that his eyes were unsteady, like those of a drunken man.

Afterwards, while Muoth was changing , I went to see the conductor.

"Tell me," I asked, "is Muoth ill? It seems to me that he is keeping himself going with champagne. You know that he is a friend of mine, don't you?"

He looked at me in despair. "I don't know if he is ill, but it is quite evident that he is ruining himself. He has sometimes come on stage almost drunk, and if he ever misses a drink, he acts and sings badly. He always used to have a glass of champagne before appearing, but now he never has less than a whole bottle. If you want to give him some advice — but there is little you can do.

Muoth is deliberately ruining himself."

Muoth came for me and we went to the nearest inn for supper. He was languid and taciturn again, as he had been at lunchtime, drank large quantities of a heavy red wine, for otherwise he could not sleep, and looked as if he wanted to forget at any price that there were other things in the world than his fatigue and desire for sleep.

On the way back in the cab he revived for a moment, laughed and said: "My friend, once I'm gone, you can pickle your opera. No one else but me could sing that part."

The following morning he rose late and was still tired and listless, with unsteady eyes and an ashen face. After he had had his breakfast I took him aside and had a talk with him.

"You are killing yourself," I said, both anxiously and crossly. "You revive yourself with champagne and afterwards you naturally have to pay for it. I can imagine why you are doing it, and I would not say anything if you did not have a wife. You owe it to her to be respectable and courageous, outwardly and inwardly."

"Really!" He smiled weakly, evidently amused by my vehemence. "And what does she owe me? Does she act courageously? She stays with her father and leaves all alone. Why should I pull myself together when she doesn't? People already know there is nothing between us any longer and you know it too, but just the same I have to sing and entertain people. I can't do it with the feeling of emptiness and disgust which I have about everything, particularly about art."

"All the same, you must turn over a new leaf, Muoth! It is not as if drinking made you happy! You are absolutely wretched! If singing is too much for you at the moment, ask for a leave of absence; you would obtain it immediately. You are not dependent on the money that you earn by singing. Go into the mountains, or to the sea, or wherever you like, and get well again. And give up that stupid drinking! It is not only stupid, it is cowardly. You know that quite well."

He smiled at that. "Oh yes," he said coolly. "You go and dance a waltz sometime! It would do you good, believe me! Don't always be thinking about your stupid leg. That is just imagination!"

"Stop it," I cried angrily. "You know quite well that is different. I would very much like to dance if I could, but I can't. But you can quite well pull yourself together and behave more sensibly. You must definitely give up drinking."

"Definitely! My dear Kuhn, you make me laugh. It is just as difficult for me to alter and give up drinking as it is for you to dance. I must cling to the things that still keep up my spirits. Do you understand? People who drink are converted when they find something in the Salvation Army or elsewhere that gives them more satisfaction and is more enduring. There was once something like that for me, namely women, but I can no longer take an interest in any other woman since she has been mine and has now forsaken me, so — "

"She has not forsaken you! She will come back. She is only ill."

"That is what you think and that is what she thinks herself, I know, but she will not come back. When a ship is going to sink, the rats abandon it beforehand. Obviously, they do not know that the ship is going under; they only feel touched by a slight sensation of nausea and run away, no doubt with the intention of soon returning."

"Oh, don't talk like that! You have often despaired in your life and yet things have turned out all right."

"True! That is because I found some consolation or narcotic. Sometimes it was a woman, sometimes a good friend — yes, you too once helped me that way — at other times it was music or applause in the theater. But now these things no longer give me pleasure and that is why I drink. I could never sing without first having a couple of drinks, but now I cannot even think, talk, live or feel tolerably well without first having a couple of drinks. Anyway, you must stop lecturing me, whatever you think. The same situation arose once before, about twelve years ago. Someone lectured me then also and did not let me alone. It was about a girl, and by a coincidence it was my best friend — "

"And then?"

"Then I was obliged to throw him out. After that I did not have a friend for a long time — as a matter of fact not until you came along."

"That is evident."

"Is it?" he said mildly. "Well, you can drop me too. But I will say that I would be sorry if you left me in the lurch just now. I am attached to you and I have also thought of something to give you pleasure."

"Have you? What is it?"

"Listen. You are fond of my wife, or at least you used to be, and I am also fond of her, very much so. Now let us have a celebration tonight, just you and me, in her honor. There is a special reason for it. I have had a portrait of her painted; she had to visit the artist frequently earlier in the year and I often went with her. The portrait was almost ready when she went away. The artist wanted her to sit once more, but I grew tired of waiting and ordered the portrait to be delivered as it is. That was a week ago, and now it is framed and arrived here yesterday. I should have shown it to you at once, but it would be better to have a celebration for it. It would not be much good without a few glasses of champagne. How could I enjoy it otherwise? Do you agree?"

I sensed the emotion and even the tears behind his joking manner and I cheerfully agreed, although I was not really in the mood for it.

We made preparations for the celebration in honor of the woman who seemed so completely lost to him, as she was in fact to me.

"Can you remember which flowers she likes?" he asked me. "I don't know anything about flowers or what they are called. She always had some white and yellow ones, and also some red ones. Do you know what they are?"

"Yes, I know some of them. Why?"

"You must buy some. Order a cab. I

must go up to town in any case. We shall act as if she were here."

He did many other things that made me realize how deeply and incessantly he had thought about Gertrude. It made me both happy and sad to observe this. Because of her, he no longer kept a dog and he lived alone, he who previously could never be without women for long. He had had a portrait of her painted. He asked me to buy the flowers she liked. It was as if he had taken off a mask and I saw a child's face behind the hard, selfish features.

"But," I objected, "we ought to look at the portrait now, or this afternoon. It is always better to look at pictures by daylight."

"Does it matter? You can look at it again tomorrow. I hope it is a good painting, but in truth that is not so important; we just want to look at her."

After a meal we traveled to town and made some purchases, first of all flowers, a large bunch of chrysanthemums, a basket of roses and two bunches of white lilac. He also had the sudden idea of having a large quantity of flowers sent to Gertrude in R.

"There is something lovely about flowers," he said thoughtfully. "I can understand Gertrude being fond of them. I like them too, but I cannot take the trouble to look after anything like that. When there is no woman to attend to them, they always seem to me to be uncared for and do not really give me pleasure."

In the evening I found that the new portrait had been placed in the music room and was covered with a silk cloth. We had had an excellent meal, after which Muoth wished first to hear the wedding prelude. When I had played it, he uncovered the portrait and we stood facing it for a while in silence. Gertrude had been painted full-length in a light summer dress, and her bright eyes looked across at us trustfully from the portrait. It was some time before we could look at each other and take each other's hand. Heinrich filled two glasses with Rhine wine, bowed to the portrait, and we drank to the woman about whom we were both thinking. Then he carefully picked up the picture and carried it out.

I asked him to sing something, but he did not wish to.

"Do you remember," he said smiling, "how we spent an evening together before my wedding? Now I am a bachelor once more and we shall again try to cheer ourselves up with a couple of drinks and have a little pleasure. Your friend Teiser ought to be here; he knows how to make merry better than you and I. Give him my regards when you are back home. He can't bear me, but just the same — "

With the steadily maintained cheerfulness that had been a characteristic of his best hours, he began to chat and to remind me of things that had taken place in the past, and I was surprised at how much he remembered. Even casual little things that I thought he had long forgotten remained in his memory. He had not even forgotten the very first evening I had spent at his house, together with Marian and Kranzl, and the way we had quarrelled. Only about Gertrude did he remain silent. He did not mention the period in which she had come into our lives and I was glad that he did not do so.

I felt pleased about this unexpected enjoyable evening and let him help himself liberally to the good wine without admonishing him. I knew how rare these moods were with him, and how he cherished and clung to them when they occasionally came, and they never did come without the aid of wine. I also knew that this mood would not last long and that tomorrow he would again be irritable and unapproachable. Nevertheless it gave me a feeling of well-being and almost cheerfulness to listen to his clever, thoughtful, although perhaps contradictory observations. While talking , he occasionally directed one of his attractive glances at me, which he did only in such hours as these, and they were like the glances of one who had just awakened from a dream.

Once, when he was silent and sat thinking, I began to tell him what my theosophist friend had said to me about the sickness of lonely people.

"Oh," he said good-humoredly, "and I suppose you believed him. You should have become a theologian."

"Why do you say that ? After all, there may be something in it."

"Oh, of course. Wise men continually demonstrate from time to time that everything is only imagination. Do you know, I often used to read such books in the past and I can tell you that they are of no use, absolutely no use. All that these philosophers write about is only a game; perhaps they comfort themselves with it. One philosopher preaches individualism because he can't bear his contemporaries, and another socialism because he can't endure being alone. It may be that our feeling of loneliness is an illness, but one can't do anything about it. Somnambulism is also an illness, and that is why a fellow suffering from it does in fact stand at the edge of a roof, and when someone calls out to him, he falls and breaks his neck."

"That is quite different."

"Maybe. I won't say I am right. I only

mean that one doesn't get anywhere with wisdom. There are only two kinds of wisdom; all the rest is just idle talk."

"Which two kinds of wisdom do you mean?"

"Well, either the world is bad and worthless, as Buddhists and Christians preach, in which case one must do penance and renounce everything — I believe one can obtain peace of mind in this way — ascetics do not have such a hard life as people think. Or else the world and life are good and right — then one can just take part in it and afterwards die peacefully, because it is finished."

"What do you believe in yourself?"

"It is no use asking that. Most people believe in both, dependent on the weather, their health, and whether they have money in their purses or not. And those who really believe do not live in accordance with their beliefs. That is how it is with me too. For instance, I believe as Buddha did that life is not worthwhile, but I live for things that appeal to my senses as if this is the most important thing to do. If only it was more satisfying!"

It was not yet late when we finished. As we went through the adjoining room, where only a single electric light was burning, Muoth took my arm and stopped me, switched on all the lights and removed the cover from Gertrude's portrait, which stood there. We looked once more at her dear, sweet face; then he placed the cover over the picture again and switched out the lights. He came with me to my room and put a couple of magazines on the table in case I should want to read. Then he took my hand and said quietly: "Good night, my dear fellow!"

I went to bed and lay awake for about half an hour, thinking about him. It had moved me and made me feel ashamed to hear how faithfully he remembered all the small events of our friendship. He, who found it difficult to extend friendship, clung to those he cared for more fervently than I had thought.

After that I fell asleep and had confused dreams about Muoth, my opera and Mr. Lohe. When I awoke, it was still night. I had been awakened by a fright that had nothing to do with my dreams. I saw the dull gray of approaching dawn framed by the window and had a feeling of deep anguish. I sat up in bed and tried to shake off my sleep and think clearly.

Then there were heavy rapid knocks on my door. I sprang out of bed and opened it. It was cold and I had not yet switched on the light. The servant stood outside, scantily dressed, and stared at me anxiously with eyes full of terror.

''Will you please come?'' he whispered, panting. "There has been an accident."

I put on a dressing gown and followed the young man down the stairs. He opened a door, stood back and let me enter. In the room there was a small cane table with a candelabrum on it in which three thick candles were burning. By the side of the table there was a disordered bed and in it, lying on his face, was my friend Heinrich Muoth.

"We must turn him around," I said softly.

The servant did not trust himself to do it. "I will fetch a doctor immediately," he said stammering.

But I compelled him to pull himself together and we turned the recumbent man over. I looked at my friend's face, which was white and drawn. His shirt was covered with blood, and when we put him down and covered him up again, his mouth twitched slightly and his eyes could no longer see.

The servant than began to tell me excitedly what had happened but I did not want to know anything. When the doctor arrived, Muoth was already dead. In the morning I sent a telegram to Imthor. Then I returned to the silent house, sat by the dead man's bed, listened to the wind in the trees outside, and only then realized how fond I had been of this unfortunate man. I could not mourn for him; his death had been easier than his life.

In the evening I stood at the railway station and saw old Mr. Imthor step out of the train, followed by a tall woman dressed in black. I took them back with me to the dead man, who had now been dressed and placed on his bier among the flowers of the previous day. Gertrude stooped and kissed his pale lips.

When we stood beside his grave, I saw a tall, attractive woman with a tear-stained face, who held roses in her hand and stood alone, and when I looked across at her curiously, I saw that it was Lottie. She nodded to me and smiled. But Gertrude had not wept; she looked straight ahead of her, attentively and steadfast, in the light rain scattered about by the wind, and held herself like a young tree supported by firm roots. But it was only self-restraint; two days later, when she was unpacking Muoth's flowers, which had meantime arrived at her house, she broke down and we did not see her for a long time.

Chapter Nine

My grief, too, only came to the fore later and, as is always the case, I thought of numerous instances when I had been unjust to my dead friend. Well, he had inflicted the worst things upon himself, and not only his death. I meditated for a long time about these things and could not find anything vague or incomprehensible about his fate, and yet it was all horrible and a mockery. It was no different with my own life, with Gertrude's and that of many others. Fate was not kind, life was capricious and terrible, and there was no good or reason in nature. But there is good and reason in us, in human beings, with whom fortune plays, and we can be stronger than nature and fate, if only for a few hours. And we can draw close to one another in times of need, understand and love one another, and live to comfort each other.

And sometimes, when the black depths are silent, we can do even more. We can then be gods for moments, stretch out a commanding hand and create things which were not there before and which, when they are created, continue to live without us. Out of sounds, words and other frail and worthless things, we can construct playthings — songs and poems full of meaning, consolation and goodness, more beautiful and enduring than the grim sport of fortune and destiny. We can keep the spirit of God in our hearts and, at times, when we are full of him, he can appear in our eyes and our words, and also talk to others who do not know or do not wish to know him. We cannot evade life's course, but we can school ourselves to be superior to fortune and also to look unflinchingly upon the most painful things.

So during the years that have passed since Heinrich Muoth's death I have brought him to life again a thousand times, and have been able to talk to him more wisely and affectionately than I did when he was alive. And as time passed, my old mother died, and also pretty Brigitte Teiser, who, after years of waiting and giving the wound time to heal, married a musician and did not outlive her first confinement.

Gertrude has overcome the pain she suffered when she received our flowers as a greeting and plea from the dead. I do not often speak to her about it although I see her every day, but I believe that she looks back on the springtime of her life as on a distant valley seen during a journey a long time ago, and not a lost garden of Eden. She has regained her strength and serenity and also sings again, but since that cold kiss on the dead man's lips, she has never kissed another man. Once or twice, during the course of the years, when her spirit had recovered and her being radiated the old charm, my thoughts traveled along the old forbidden paths and I asked myself: why not? But I already knew the answer, that no change could be made in our relationship with each other. She is my friend, and after lonely, restless periods, when I emerge from my silence with a song or a sonata, it belongs first and foremost to us both.

Muoth was right. On growing old, one becomes more contented than in one's youth, which I will not therefore revile, for in all my dreams I hear my youth like a wonderful song which now sounds more harmonious than it did in reality, and even sweeter.

The publishers hope that this Large Print Book has brought you pleasurable reading. Each title is designed to make the text as easy to see as possible. If you wish a complete list of the Large Print Books we have published, ask at your local library or write directly to:

G. K. Hall & Co.
70 Lincoln St.
Boston, Mass. 02111